NIRVANA

ON NINTH STREET

Other works by Susan Sherman

Poetry

Areas of Silence

With Anger/With Love

Women Poems Love Poems

We Stand Our Ground
(with Kimiko Hahn & Gale Jackson)

Barcelona Journal

Casualties of War

The Light that Puts an End to Dreams

Essays, Poems, Short Fiction

The Color of the Heart:
Writing from Struggle and Change 1959-1990

Memoir

America's Child: A Woman's Journey Through the Radical Sixties

Translation

Shango de Ima
(An adaptation from Spanish of a Cuban play by Pepe Carril)

NIRVANA

ON NINTH STREET

SUSAN SHERMAN

Afterword by Rona L. Holub
Photographs by Colleen McKay

San Antonio, Texas
2014

ISBN: 978-1-60940-407-9 (paperback original)

E-books:
ePub: 978-1-60940-408-6
Mobipocket/Kindle: 978-1-60940-409-3
Library PDF: 978-1-60940-410-9

Wings Press
627 E. Guenther
San Antonio, Texas 78210
Phone/fax: (210) 271-7805
On-line catalogue and ordering:
www.wingspress.com

Wings Press books are distributed to the trade by
Independent Publishers Group
www.ipgbook.com

Cataloging In Publication:

Sherman, Susan, 1939-
  [Short Stories. Selections]
  Nirvana on Ninth Street / by Susan Sherman ; photographs by Colleen McKay ; afterword by Rona L. Holub.
      p. cm.
   ISBN 978-1-60940-407-9 (pbk. : alk. paper) -- ISBN 978-1-60940-408-6 (ePub eBook) -- ISBN 978-1-60940-409-3 (Kindle eBook) -- ISBN 978-1-60940-410-9 (library pdf eBook)
   1. East Village (New York, N.Y.)--Fiction. I. Title.
   PS3569.H434 N57 2014
   813'.54

CONTENTS

¡y aventada mi memoria
llegaré desnuda al mar!

and escaping my memory
I will come naked to the sea.

—Gabriela Mistral

PROLOGUE

She *wondered if birds enjoy flying, or if they do so unconscious of soaring through the wind. She wondered if birds fly as most humans walk, solely to get from one place to another. She had meant to ask, but was constantly being distracted. There was the light to be tended as it grew and dimmed, and the sound of the waves to be fine tuned. She wandered around the great expanse of the heavens as if it were her own backyard, as if she had a backyard. But what did that matter when the sky was the limit, when everyone else was firmly tied to the earth, old 'terra firma,' but her.*

If I take myself in hand, Rachel thought to herself, maybe I can reach past the boundaries of the universe. Who knows what worlds I might discover on the other side, on the edges of nowhere, on the borders of tomorrow.

Thoughts like this often drifted through her mind now, but vanished almost as soon as they appeared. Rachel was an optimist at heart. She thought in triangles, not circles or squares as most others did. Her mind took sharp turns, darting from one place to another. She cornered years, taking them at high speed, a bit recklessly perhaps, but ever confident, always in control. Whenever she could, she avoided obtuse angles, dull minds and imaginations.

She liked danger.

Can I really be what I imagine myself to be? Rachel wondered aloud. It had been so much easier when she was young, so much easier to believe. Preferring the wondrous to the down-to-earth, she had hated stories of little girls and boys her own age who lived in towns like hers, or even farther away in unknown lands. No matter how foreign, the textbook tales were always peopled with the thoughts and actions of the children who lived near her, who suffocated her with their noise and demands. She hated mundane explanations, preferred mystery and magic, times far distant, past or future. As much as humanly possible, Rachel avoided the here and now.

But age had crept up on her, had rounded bends she never took, had hit her in the belly, the solar plexus, dented her belief.

There was nowhere left to go, but up.

And so she soared. Let them think what they would. Let them search from here until tomorrow, from there until never. They would not find her, lost in blue, leaving their days and lives behind…

Ninth Street & Avenue B

Rachel lived in a small, rectangular apartment with eight windows that occupied the entire top floor of a three-story building located in the back of a tenement on East Ninth Street in Manhattan. Two of her windows fronted a concrete courtyard; two, a fenced-in backyard filled with garbage of every description. Two side windows faced an alley, while the remaining windows came within three feet of the building next door. Rachel lived there with a calico cat named Jezebel who was the talk of the neighborhood for her prowess in catching rats twice her size.

For months now, each time she passed in front of the antique mirror framed by gilt angels that graced the most prominent location in her living room, she would pause and look at herself, measuring her present stocky five-foot-five frame with its wisps of graying hair against the tall slender woman with the surfeit of gleaming chestnut locks who had first moved into Ninth Street— was it almost fifty years ago? She watched the years shadow her face with a sinking sensation in the pit of her stomach, with a fear that belied her calmness, the cool exterior with which other people saw her approach her everyday affairs.

Buddhists believe Nirvana unachievable until one is able to find peace in the present moment, to cease longing to be somewhere else, someone else. For Rachel, that was impossible. Most often she wished desperately to be anywhere but where she was, burdened as she always seemed by the smallest details of daily life: what vegetables to eat for dinner, what to wear or wash or discard, the mail that had to be answered, the accumulation of years that waited to be sorted, the fear of throwing away the one essential document on which everything would depend at some unknown date in the near or distant future.

Rachel was a cipher, on the one hand simple, on the other too difficult for even her to fathom. One year she strayed and became lost to herself. She remembered as a child being pulled under by the tide and finally deposited, frightened and gasping for air, on a windless beach, bleeding from a dozen cuts caused by the sharp protrusions of stone the relentless waves had washed her across. Even so she loved the sea, loved its sound, was glad when night came, and she could hear it without distraction. The patience of it, moving endlessly across sand, driven by wind and tide and moon. Never wavering, never stopping, never the same. The endless ebb and flow of difference.

If she had not chosen, or been chosen—who knows which?— to drift through the air, to cleanse the heavens, the sea would have been her home. Not the surface, but the depth of it. Down where it was dark and green. She could never understand why fish had such a multitude of colors in a place where there was no light. She wondered how they must feel when caught, if the last thing they recognize, as they lie gasping for the water that is their air, is the blazing light of the sun. She wondered if that was why there were so many tales of a blazing white light signaling the approach of death. Was it merely the remnants of an archaic memory, when we too lived beneath the waves, never seeing the light until, with our last breath, we floated finally lifeless on the surface of the water? A dream of heaven that ties us to our past?

Every morning at exactly 8:35, Rachel fed Jezebel, watered her plants and fixed herself a cup of blackberry-flavored tea and one piece of crisply toasted bread. Rachel believed in schedules. How else could she accomplish all she had to do? By 9:10, as soon as she had finished all her morning chores, she would stand by the front window of her house, the one that faced the concrete courtyard, and checking first to see that the sun was in the correct position, would counsel the clouds to make sure that no two were alike. In her universe, imitation was taboo.

Rachel had always wanted to be a character in a novel, preferably a period piece from the Thirties or Forties, so when her movie was made, the score would be the music she loved, the old songs, melodic, romantic, with just a trace of sadness. People would walk out of the theater humming her music, and thereafter, every time they heard it, would remember her. Rachel wanted someone to write dialogue for her, so she would always say something clever, would always know what to say, would never have to stop and ruminate, sometimes a whole day, only to find it too late to confront the person who was no longer there. She wanted to live a plot that was simple, where choices would be made for her and would always be the right choice, insuring that even if the ending were tragic, she would emerge a heroine, beautiful in courage and determination.

But she knew she was, finally, only an aging woman with dreams that sometimes carried her beyond the ordinary. She was not a character in a novel, romantic or otherwise. She was not the heroine of a movie, happy or tragic.

The night before she turned seventy, Rachel dreamt Ninth Street in the old days: PS 37 at the corner, a massive brick structure with two sides that jutted out like a grotesque inverted smile, a u-shape facing the street, waiting to devour the children crowding its hungry path; the grocery store simply named *Grocery Store* squeezed between two apartment buildings in the middle of the block that dispensed sausage, pierogi, and cigarettes. It was a community store owned by a neighborhood couple, Helen and her husband George, and staffed by Rachel's Ukrainian neighbors Passion and her sister Peace, who worked there until she was frightened by the riots of '68 and went west to work for Sadie Goldstein, the owner of the deli on Second Avenue, taking over Sadie's position when she finally retired.

Rachel dreamt she looked in the antique mirror framed by gilt angels and saw herself young again, careless of hair, the necessity of make-up and excuses. She dreamt that Jennifer was back in her old apartment, one wall covered with sketches her downstairs neighbor Alison had drawn one night when she was high on LSD, drawings whose grotesque figures were wrapped in greens and purples and blues, like Rachel's ocean.

She dreamt that she was lying next to Jennifer, that she was fixing Norma her favorite pasta with pesto sauce and garlic bread, that she was greeting Alison's lover Solomon (one of the many who passed through Alison's welcoming threshold) on his way to the garage on Third Street and Avenue C to scavenge for pieces of iron and tin to use in the construction of his intricate sculptures. Rachel dreamt she was young and her life was before her, that the shadows that haunted her apartment, shading it from light and warmth, once more had flesh and blood. She dreamt she had at long last found the intimacy she so desperately craved.

Rachel missed Norma. She missed Sadie and Jennifer and Solomon and Paul and Alberto. She even missed crotchety old Mrs. Mitchell who had made life on Ninth Street impossible for Jill and her canary Peter only to find her existence empty without them. Rachel missed Margaret Hansen who had died of a stroke with all of their histories laid out before her in strange and intricate configurations. She missed her old friends and lovers and everything she had lost. She missed the future she felt she had betrayed.

She felt if she could recall her friends, even people she had disliked and dismissed when they had been beside her, their lives might become part of hers. Rachel knew that she no less than Sadie, the inveterate neighborhood confidant, lived through other people's stories. Or maybe she had all along made her story theirs.

SOLOMON

Solomon lived on the other side of the tracks. Or more precisely, he lived east of Avenue C which was, in some circles, considered the same thing. His was a neighborhood that one ventured into cautiously, the stated line of demarcation being Tompkins Square Park, even though some of the blocks—like the one Rachel lived on—were still considered relatively safe.

Solomon's parents had moved to the Lower East Side from South Carolina when he was still a small child, sacrificing the warm days and nights and known limitations of the segregated rural South of the Fifties for the freedom and frigid winters of New York City streets. After graduating from high school, Solomon rented an apartment only two blocks from them and then, much to their dismay, announced his intention to become a sculptor.

Solomon loved the smell of the molten steel he twisted into forms and shapes that resembled the chaotic ramblings of his imagination. The images he thought in, even in his dreams, although vaguely figurative, were far from realistic. They followed the lines and patterns of the barren twigs and dusty roads of his youth, the bantering of his mother, the harsh echo of his father's footsteps, the fear that had driven his family northward, that had finally filled him so full that it catapulted him outside his self-imposed boundaries into the cafes and bars that ringed the park, into the words and gestures of the painters and poets and students and musicians that frequented their corridors. It was from them Solomon learned first to draw and then to paint.

But that wasn't enough for him. He still felt stifled by memories, the small dank apartment he had grown up in, the endless arguments, his own confusion. So he began to collect scrap metal, rummaging through garbage cans, empty lots, gas station discards, the impromptu dumps that dotted the neighborhood. At first he made his new creations with his bare hands, and then one summer evening a sympathetic mechanic loaned him an acetylene torch, and Solomon knew he had at last found the materials and method to express the rage and despair he had held so long inside him.

He filled his sculptures with it, coated the blackened surfaces of the scarred skin of his work with it, as if he were pulling off pieces of himself, covering the jagged frames of his "people" with his own dark flesh, with his marrow, his blood.

Because that's what his sculptures were to him, even though no one else could see it—people. His mother and father; his two brothers; Beatrice, the sister who had died in childbirth; the boys he had fought with before he grew too large for them to bully; the Puerto Rican boy he had almost killed one night in a drunken brawl over a girl neither of them really wanted; the adults, black and white alike, who still intimidated him with their doubts and recriminations—all these shaped themselves at the end of his torch as he created and re-created them in an endless processional.

His sculptures were small, no more than a foot in height, sized to fit the dimensions of his kitchen studio. Sometimes he splattered their bodies with brilliant color, sometimes they were polished to a gleaming silver and chrome, but more often he left them bare, gray and blackened, naked and vulnerable before the intensity of his flame.

Solomon's father, almost six feet tall, slender of build, could hardly be described as a little man, but his son towered above him, tall and massive of bone by the time he was sixteen. His father had nicknamed him Solomon, joking that what he lacked in wit, he made up in size. His size both got him into and out of trouble. Enemies were reluctant to attack him, passers-by hesitant to confront him. Consequently, Solomon labored under a dangerous delusion—he believed he led a charmed life.

CJ was Solomon's best and only real friend. In many ways, CJ was the exact opposite of Solomon. He was short, slight of build, but nonetheless quite strong. He counted success in dollars and cents. Unlike Solomon's parents, CJ's mother and father had both been born in Harlem. His father ran a small tobacco store, and CJ had grown up on a well-tended middle class block on 138th

Street. He admired his father and dreamed of one day having a business of his own.

"Solomon," he would say, "with all your talent what do you really have you can bank on? Bank on, man, that's the ticket in this world. Money equals power, man. Money equals power."

He would end his lectures with a gruff laugh, giving Solomon the high sign and a playful push.

No matter what CJ said to him, Solomon never got mad. In fact, CJ had never seen Solomon get really mad at anyone. Solomon could stand for hours at the northeast corner entrance to Tompkins Square Park waving his arms, railing about the state of the nation, the CIA conspiracy, the racist neighborhood police, drug dealers, the FBI, filthy streets, crummy schools, pollution—brandishing the morning paper like a defiant flag. But CJ had never seen him actually yell at anyone. His eyes were always turned to heaven, as if it were God he was lecturing; as if God, as far as Solomon was concerned, was a criminal not even the Republican National Committee could match.

CJ and Solomon did share some things, otherwise they could not have been such good friends. They shared a love of making things with their hands, of feeling cold, hard materials grow into life. CJ had a passion for wood; he loved to build things. But his creations, unlike those of Solomon, were practical—chairs, tables, bookshelves, windowsills, kitchen cabinets. He could take pieces of wood that had been discarded as useless and find purpose and meaning behind their splintered shells. He dreamed one day of having his own construction company, of expanding his talents to rebuilding rooms, apartments, even houses. Of taking what was spoiled and making something new and useful of it.

CJ and Solomon also shared the same girlfriend. Her name was Alison. Alison was one of Rachel's closest neighbors. She occupied the basement and first floor of their little back-house building. Alison was a painter. Every morning Rachel watched Alison usher her two girls—aged five and seven—out the front door of their adjoined stairway, after which Alison sometimes waved Rachel down to her apartment to share a cup of coffee and the morning's gossip. Often they would go down one more flight of stairs to the basement to view Alison's new work.

Alison had left her husband the year before due to irreconcilable differences—he wanted her to assume the life of a respectable Long Island matron. She had a different idea of what she wanted her life to be like, and it didn't include suburban PTA meetings. As much as Solomon wanted to be a sculptor, she wanted to be a painter, so she had moved to Manhattan with her children and their two cats, Citrus and Cyrus—one was orange, the other male.

Unlike Solomon, whose motivation for painting was rage, Alison's was humor. She felt all her life she had wanted, but had never been allowed, to laugh. She felt her life had been punctuated by punch lines that fell flat, not because they weren't funny, but because their audience had no sense of humor. And so she went in search of the perfect joke and an audience that could appreciate it.

Her paintings were large, populated by balloon-like figures that seemed to float in space. Her colors were bright—she almost always stuck to primary tones. As an artist, her paintings were a direct contrast to the sharp, jagged edges of Solomon's imagination. But where his rage formed the skin of his sculptures, leaving him as a person childlike and benign, her paintings left her a person devoid of humor. It was as if the two of them drained their souls into their work, leaving them, as people, reverse images of their creations.

CJ and Solomon had met one day by accident at Alison's apartment and, instead of becoming bitter rivals, had become close friends. Neither's relationship with Alison was particularly deep, a level of emotion she reciprocated. They enjoyed her company, and she enjoyed theirs. CJ was handy with tools and broken things. Solomon amused her and, more important, her two small children. He would sit with them for hours, telling them stories, playing nonsense games with small metal toys he made for them.

Sometimes Alison questioned if it was her he came to see, or whether her company gave him a chance to be with people he could really relate to—small people, like the small figures with which he decorated his life. Oddly enough, he seemed happier when CJ was there, and she began to wonder whether she and CJ represented to him the parents, or at least the older brother and sister, he needed to fill his life. People who accepted him, unlike his own parents, unlike his own brothers, so close in distance, yet so far from being able to give him the understanding he craved.

Solomon had an aversion to drugs. It was built both on his own natural disposition—he had tried marijuana once or twice and had found it harsh and abrasive, his world already having enough sharp edges—and on a subconscious longing for CJ's approval.

For CJ, drugs belonged to the world of his adolescence, an environment without discipline, solidity. He craved stability in much the same way others crave excitement.

For Alison, drugs were the staff of life. She thrived on amphetamine, the rush it gave her, the energy it generated. For her, marijuana cleared the haze that grayed her world. Alison did not consider herself an addict. She was, rather, a connoisseur, taking her pleasure at will, not under any compulsion other than that of occasional triumph, and delight.

That is until someone gave her LSD.

LSD was, for her, the ultimate high, an ecstasy of color and energy. Soon she needed it to complete her day. She needed it to complete the lines that made up her world. Without it, her universe seemed full of blank spaces, like a puzzle that made no sense.

For CJ, LSD was trouble, and trouble was the last thing he needed. He loved Alison in his own way and tried to get her to see the fragility of the substitutions she was making, but it was useless. The consequent pressure on Solomon was enormous. CJ began pushing him to leave Alison, while she held out enthusiastic promises of sharing a new and wondrous vision with him.

Solomon didn't think much of her promises. He found her friends childish and stupid. He cared about her. He depended on her, but he also depended on CJ. CJ's stability grounded his creativity. CJ was a "brother" who understood where he had come from, where his future lay. He knew CJ would never desert him, his friendship was as solid as the oak cabinets he loved to make.

Solomon felt trapped. He couldn't work. He couldn't sleep. His days and nights took on the jagged metal forms of his sculptures, tearing at him with their demands. Finally he decided he would leave with CJ to help him in his new construction business in East Harlem, but he would not stop seeing Alison, and he would, at least once, take "acid" with her.

Alison was delighted at his acquiescence, and their next evening together was almost like the old days when they first met, with supper, nondescript chatter, gossip about the few people they knew in common. He inquired about her art, she asked about his. After dessert they took sugar cubes saturated with LSD and made love, and as the drug began to take effect, Solomon began to feel a strange glow, a growing warmth. It was a feeling he often had after making love, but this was different, it was tangible. He felt himself getting denser, falling into himself, as simultaneously he had the feeling he was growing lighter and more transparent. He had never seemed so light. He realized how weighted down he had always felt by the girth of his body, how his body enclosed him like the huge leather jacket his brother had gotten for him the year he turned fifteen, the jacket he had hated, but worn for years, afraid to hurt his brother's feelings, because it made him feel even larger than he was, when he wanted so much to be small, to blend in.

He began to feel warm and chilled at the same time. He got out of bed and put on his clothes. They gave an outline to a body that kept trying to come apart, drift away. Despite his clothes, his body was disappearing, one limb at a time. First his arm, and then a finger, and then his right ear. He laughed as his cheek vanished, and then his chin, and then his left ear. He now had three fingers on his left hand, four on his right. The heat increased. He felt he was burning. His body had all but evaporated.

Suddenly, understanding exploded inside him. It was not metal that formed the material of his art. It was not metal that shaped his tiny figures. It was the fire he used to create them.

It was flame he desired.

He felt he had to get to his studio. He hadn't a moment to lose. Alison was lying stretched out on the bed, motionless. He knelt down beside her. He tried to explain to her what had happened to him, that he had to leave, that he had to return to his studio. Her eyes half closed, she silently nodded her head. It was impossible to know if she understood, if she even heard him, but he couldn't wait to find out. Hastily gathering the odds and ends he had left scattered around and throwing them into his worn duffel bag, he bolted out of her room in a fury of inspiration and dread.

It was two in the morning when he arrived at his studio. The night was chill. The streets were empty. He felt, as he turned his key in the lock, something miraculous had happened.

As he opened the door, he knew he was right. His studio was alive. Each piece of metal radiated a different color and voice. His creations were crying out to him. What was it they wanted? He couldn't make out what they were saying, their voices barely a whisper. Speak louder, he encouraged them, knowing it was within his power in this place to grant them anything they wished.

Their voices swelled. Yes, now he could hear. Now he could hear them. They were begging him to once again bathe them in the flame of life, to exhale his warmth, to cover them. They were pleading with him, in the voice of his preacher when he was a child so long ago in the South, to let them be consumed by the fire of divinity, to restore them to a perfect pristine existence.

And he could. He could do that for them. In the radiance of his joy, in his love for them, he could purify them. He could cleanse them of the filth of the streets, of their memories of loss and abuse, of violence and terror.

He took his torch, and the flame that came from it was revelation, it was salvation, and he bathed his creatures in it, and he bathed his paintings and drawings in it, and he washed his worktable and chairs and windows and ceiling with it.

He took his torch and with it he washed away his longing and his anger. He washed away his love for CJ and Alison. He cleansed himself of his memories of his mother, and brothers, of his dead sister, of his father.

And then he turned his torch on his own hands and, like Pontius Pilate, he washed himself clean.

CAROLINE

When **Caroline** entered a room all conversation stopped. She affected people that way. She couldn't help it. It wasn't the way she looked. She actually was fairly ordinary looking, with hazel eyes and shoulder length brown hair parted precisely in the middle. An attractive, but not striking woman, everything about her was neatly centered—her age, weight, height. It was just a sense people had about her, that she was a person you had to be careful around.

It was true Caroline couldn't tolerate anyone being angry at her. Any harsh word would make her tremble for hours. Any slight terrified her, made her embarrassed, ashamed. Maybe that was what made people so cautious. Maybe they felt this reticence on her part.

Rachel was Caroline's dearest friend. Rachel knew all the ways Caroline's mind twisted, could walk the sidewalk of her emotions, navigate the rambling nature of her reflections. Rachel seemed to understand everything in that far-off, spaced-out way of hers.

Caroline often felt Rachel was looking past her, gazing at some scene only she could see, but it didn't make her uncomfortable to be looked at like that. She knew she would never have to fear Rachel's anger because nothing was ever directed at her. She liked it that way.

In the many years Caroline had known Rachel, the world they lived in had subtly changed. A huge building on Second Avenue which had first been a Loews Movie Emporium, then the Fillmore East—a popular venue for Rock, in all its various Sixties and Seventies forms—and then The Saint, an infamous disco, was now a bank. It seemed to Caroline the appropriate signifier for the end of the century. The millennium would be ushered in not by fire and flames, but a subtler Armageddon—The New York First Federal Savings and Loan.

Caroline was a tailor by trade. She had learned the skill from her father, who had learned the skill from his wife, who had learned the skill from her mother. An immigrant, it was her father's only source of income at the beginning of a century when Jewish scholars from Russia and Poland were hardly valued for their intellectual skills. How interesting, Caroline mused, that almost one hundred years later things have changed so little. Here I am, a scholar at heart, sewing buttons and hems for a living—along with an occasional dress or fancy shirt for a wedding or funeral. My clothes are like bookends, holding together the beginnings and endings of life.

She was pleased by the tiny stitches she still knew how to make, even though most of her work now days was done on an old Singer sewing machine she had purchased at a flea market almost a dozen years before. Everything was needed yesterday it seemed. Everyone was in such a hurry, such a rush to get—where?

Certainly not here, Caroline smiled. I like sewing by hand, she thought. The pleasure in knowing there's a little of me in every stitch. That every stitch is slightly different, unique. That it's my fingers and not a machine drawing thread ever so carefully through the thick, unyielding cloth.

Caroline was an expert on cloth. She could tell by touch alone the name of a fabric, sometimes even where it was from. She could feel color as well as texture. Running her fingers up and down large bolts of cloth, eyes closed, she could classify stripes and checks, solid colors and bold hues, green and gold, red and purple, blue and every shade of gray, all the colors of the rainbow. If the fabric were silk, she could distinguish more delicate hues—solemn flowers resting in a vase of emerald jade, the pain of the silkworm running through each thread.

I hope it is not pain that makes the fabric slide like sex between my fingers, like the softest skin beneath my hands, she thought. Thank goodness no one can read my mind, see me here eyes closed, sitting in front of my old machine, rubbing this square of cloth between my fingers. They would think me mad!

Caroline's husband Dan worked for a Salvation Army Youth Center on MacDougal Street in Greenwich Village. She smiled remembering Rachel's expression when she first told her his occupation. Maybe Rachel had expected to see him in full Salvation Army Uniform, brass buttons gleaming, playing a trombone, a character straight out of "Guys and Dolls." Her friends were always surprised when they finally met Dan, seeing instead of the figure of their imagination a man perfectly suited to Caroline—even featured, medium height, weight, usually dressed in a pair of old jeans and one of a variety of mediumsized T-shirts. Even his name, Dan, was a medium-sized name.

Caroline was proud of the work Dan did. He had rescued more than one teenager from the Village streets, had gotten more than one runaway back home or into a place they would be safe, away from drugs and alcohol and nights spent looking for something to eat or a place to sleep. The kids liked him. They called him, "Dan the Man." They trusted him, depended on him. And so did she.

Besides Dan and her sewing machine, Caroline had a dog named Ranger. Ranger was part police dog, part something undefined. He adored Caroline. He guarded her and her storefront with a vigilance that was unsurpassed. When Ranger was around, she never felt afraid.

That was why it was so unusual the first weekend in September for her to find herself in her tiny storefront shop alone. Dan had taken off for a country retreat with "his boys" on Friday for the weekend and had talked her into letting him take Ranger along. She had finally agreed, knowing how much Ranger would love the country air, the long walks in green and growing woods—even though she was reluctant to let both of her companions go at once. It was bad enough when Dan was away. With the dog gone, the house seemed doubly empty.

Caroline was so engrossed in tracing the fine lines of her stitches, the intricate twisting and turning of her thoughts—she was working on a particularly demanding pattern that evening—she never heard the almost inaudible click the door made as it was expertly jimmied open. She shivered a little from the sudden chill, not realizing it was a faint but frigid breeze coming from outside the apartment.

All she knew was that suddenly the wooden panels of the old tenement floor slammed against her face. All she knew was a sudden heaviness ramming into her back. She knew instantly there was nothing she could do as her assailant grabbed her by the neck, smashing her face over and over into the floor, crushing her nose, her mouth. She felt she was drowning in her own blood as she choked for breath, caught between the vise that was his body and the unyielding wooden floor boards, as he forced himself over and over into her, leaving her torn, defenseless, curled in a small red circle on the floor.

That was how Dan found her the next morning, unconscious, lying in a pool of urine and blood, a small emerald square of silk still clenched tightly between her fingers. He had come home to an empty apartment and thinking that she had probably fallen asleep over her work, had decided to surprise her, stopping only long enough to pick up her favorite breakfast—black coffee and a toasted bagel with butter and cream cheese—at the corner Deli.

When Rachel stopped by Caroline's store later that week, the door was locked and bolted. A neighbor told her what had happened, and she immediately called her friend at home. But there was no answer. For days she continued to stop by Caroline's apartment. But there was never an answer.

Caroline survived, at least in body. But her spirit was never the same. She didn't go back to her store, and two weeks later moved out of her apartment. She refused to speak to anyone she had known before the rape, including Rachel. She refused to pick up another piece of cloth, to sew another of her meticulous stitches.

Dan got himself transferred to a job out of the city, supervising a homeless shelter in San Francisco, and, in silence, she moved with him. And, in silence, she lived with him, until finally, in search of words, he reluctantly left her and moved on.

One evening, a dozen years later, Rachel was amazed to see her friend at work in the window of a storefront not two doors down from her original shop, bent almost double over a large piece of dull red fabric, her fingers moving slowly and carefully through a maze of thread and silk. Rachel knocked loudly on the door, which was now permanently locked, even through Ranger was back, crouched protectively around Caroline's ankles. Caroline, looking up, smiled at Rachel as if nothing had happened, as if no time had passed, and just as casually unlocked the door and waved her in.

The two old friends sat for an hour, trying to find things to say to each other. Rachel, reluctant to bring up experiences that might or might not still be traumatic; Caroline, dismayed by the fact that Rachel was no longer the friend who so conveniently looked past her.

Finally they parted, everything left unspoken. Once in awhile Rachel would stop by to say hello, but the time of their friendship had passed.

A LITTLE NIGHT MUSIC

Jill sang. Oh, how she sang! She sang in the shower, in the living room, the bedroom, while she was doing the dishes, taking out the garbage. She sang *a cappella*, to old recordings, to the radio, TV. She sang opera and jazz and popular music and, once in awhile, even attempted a little rock and roll.

Jill sang to her dog, James. She sang to her canary, Peter— she hated diminutives like the ever-popular Petey. And Peter sang back to her. Sometimes they sang in unison, an incomparable duo.

The trouble was Jill couldn't carry a tune. Somewhere between her ears and her brain and her mouth everything got mixed up. But Peter didn't care. Balanced on the edge of his perch, the white crown of his head stretched into space, his throat vibrating until it seemed it would break, Peter chirped and preened happily. Peter didn't mind what Jill sounded like as long as the joyous notes issuing from her ballooning lungs made the bars of his cage tremble and dance. Peter didn't care if Jill sang off key.

Everyone else did.

One cold December night, two weeks before Christmas, a secret tenants' meeting was held to discuss Jill. Rachel protested vehemently, but to no avail. Even though she got several other tenants to join her boycott, the gathering went ahead as scheduled. It was collectively decided Jill's attempts at virtuosity were becoming annoying—more than annoying, a positive health hazard. Old Mrs. Mitchell, a curmudgeon who lived on the floor directly above Jill, insisted that her migraines were a direct result of Jill's practicing her scales at 6 o'clock in the morning.

Every morning at precisely 5:55, Mrs. Mitchell would awaken, body tensed, waiting. And then at 6, it burst uninvited into her apartment—through the glossy parquet floor, the legs of her chest of drawers, her bedposts; through her new red night lamp, her clock radio, her knitting needles.

The noise. The pain.

Something had to be done! But what? What could possibly *be* done? In any case, it seemed only fair to let Jill know how her neighbors felt. So a polite note was drafted detailing the difficulties that arose from her vocal exercises—no one wanted to dignify the screams that issued from her well-endowed vocal chords as music. It requested that she please schedule her vocalizing at a later hour and perhaps, if it were convenient, post the schedule on her door so the other tenants would be forewarned.

Jill had learned to sing from her mother, a vocal coach who had a quite marvelous voice. To be more precise, she learned to sing by listening to her mother. After one lesson, Jill's mother realized her daughter would be wise to put her voice to better use.

But, unbeknownst to her mother, Jill persisted. Even though Jill copied exactly what it was she thought she heard her mother singing, it was much like copying with great exactitude the tones of an out-of-tune piano.

Accurate, but not pleasing.

Jill didn't understand why, as a child, when she tried to sing to her mother's friends, they would pat her on the head and say "good girl" exactly the way she would later pat her dog and say "good boy." After awhile, she began to seek out isolated places she could practice, anywhere she believed no one could hear her, where she could take the tones she heard and loved and improvise on them, embellishing them with richness and clarity and texture.

If her melodies hadn't been so out-of-tune, they would have been true masterpieces.

As it was they were jarring, perplexing. They were yowlings that sent even her poor dog James scrambling for a hiding place. Only Peter the Canary was capable of accompanying her into her private world, where the two of them could sing until it seemed their very hearts would burst.

Imagine then how shocked Jill was by the letter she received the morning after the tenants' meeting. She had no idea anyone could even hear her except Peter, much less find her vocalizing intolerable.

From that day on, Jill stopped singing.

Why couldn't she just compromise with her neighbors and schedule her concerts for a later hour? The fact was Jill slept during the day. She had always feared the night. She was afraid of waking up at two or three in the morning, the hours when everyone else was asleep, when no one was there she could call out to help her in a time of need. Because it is the waking into darkness, not the vigil in darkness, that is most frightening.

So every night she stayed up, keeping busy, waiting until the moments that promised dawn. And it was precisely at those moments that music rose from her throat, and she sang.

And Peter sang with her.

When she finally realized that her ploy had worked and Jill was silenced, Mrs. Mitchell breathed a sigh of relief. She could hardly believe her torture was ended. She couldn't remember the last time she had awakened naturally, free of pain. But after awhile something strange began to happen to her. She would awaken in the morning puzzled. By mid-afternoon, she would find herself rummaging around her apartment aimlessly, looking for the, the— what was it?—she had misplaced. It bothered her. Like a word just on the edge of remembering, a familiar word, on the tip of your tongue, yet impossibly out of reach.

Peter had forgotten how to sing alone. And so, like Jill, he too lapsed into silence. He ate and drank as usual, and even occasionally played with his cuttlebone. He looked slick and healthy as always, but it was obvious that he too was missing something. However, being smarter than Mrs. Mitchell, he knew exactly what he had lost.

The days went by as they usually do, heedless of whatever drama played itself out in whatever room or rooms filled with people or animals or birds, large or small. And when the time came, in late April, the days still alternating between being blustery and wild, or warm with spring sun, notices began to arrive confirming the tenants' worst fear. Their building was to be demolished by the city. The tenants were told they would be given moving expenses, but they had to vacate their homes. The majority of tenants led by a furious Rachel decided to fight. An emergency meeting was called for the following Saturday night, in the apartment of Mrs. Mitchell.

Jill did not attend. She had already decided to move. She had contacted her mother for temporary lodging until she could find better quarters, and three weeks later, led by an anxious James tugging at his well-worn leather leash, she left her home of over thirty years, carrying only one small suitcase and a large cage covered with an ivory embroidered scarf.

In the days that followed, it was as if a new, deeper silence seeped through the walls of Jill's old apartment, traveling like wisps of fog throughout the building. A damp silence, thick and sickly green. Sometimes near dawn, early risers, or tenants coming home late from work or partying with friends, began to swear they could hear eerie sounds issuing from the vicinity of Jill's old home. Not harsh, disjointed tones like those they remembered so well, but lovely sounds. Songs. Yes, they were not afraid to call them songs.

They swore they could hear a small bird singing once again, as it had so many times before, not to greet the dawn, but to sing farewell to the night.

RACHEL GOES SHOPPING

Two days after Jill left with James and Peter, Rachel bought a baby carriage. That might have made sense if Rachel had seen, for example, a Nineteenth Century antique lined with handmade lace, with wheels and handle twisted in tarnished metal, in her favorite second-hand store, *Elk's Trading Post* on Avenue B and Twelfth Street, where she loved to browse—particularly on days when the sky was just that color of grayish-yellow only a giant city can produce. It might have made sense if the baby carriage were a pretty oddity that would fit perfectly in a corner of her living room, filled with plants, perhaps, or other assorted trivia.

But this baby carriage was quite plain, ordinary in every sense of the word. Rachel had purchased it on Fourteenth Street in a bargain store and walked it home full of groceries and four new towels. She probably wondered herself, as she pushed it through the hot dusty streets, why she had purchased an item that would surely raise all kinds of obnoxious questions.

It would be easy to attribute some psychological motivation to her purchase. The most logical being the longing for a child, something to fill an empty space—not in her apartment, in her heart.

It would be easy, but it would be wrong.

Rachel had no secret longing to have children. She loved children, but she also loved her privacy, the quiet moments she spent reading or meticulously noting down the details of her daily routine. Rather than feeling empty, most of the time Rachel felt too full. If anything, she was moved by the compulsion to subtract, not add. Emptiness was a word that wasn't in her vocabulary.

Maybe the baby carriage wasn't for her at all. Maybe she intended it as a present, but then she would have chosen more wisely, because Rachel had excellent taste and was generous to a fault.

The truth is that these were the thoughts of neighbors and friends who saw her that day pushing and pulling by turns the over-burdened carriage up the steep stairs to her apartment. And since her stairway was in an open courtyard, it was quite a sight indeed.

"How odd she is," one neighbor whispered to the other as they met on their own stairs in the main building, steps that, unlike Rachel's, were enclosed and hidden from view.

"She gets odder every day."

The answer to the mystery of Rachel's baby carriage, however, is not really complicated. In order to understand Rachel's actions, you would have to put yourself in Rachel's place, a place free from the vicissitudes of psychological schools or neighborly concerns.

Every morning Rachel would go over her schedule, marking off the beginning and end of each event, even though they were exactly the same every day—with the exception of English lessons she gave on Wednesdays for extra money to supplement her social security payments.

Every afternoon, at precisely two o'clock, Rachel dressed for her daily walk. Being Rachel, it wasn't possible for her to take a walk without a specific purpose in mind, some necessary errand to justify her excursion. Who knows what in her past forced her to find a reason for even the most mundane activity.

The day Rachel bought the baby carriage it was hot, and she was tired and worried and decided to direct her daily walk to the Union Square Green Market. It always cheered her to see the rows of fresh fruits and vegetables, apples and strawberries, blueberries, peaches, melons, mushrooms, tomatoes and corn—sweet corn with tiny kernels still wrapped in over-lapping layers of green— and the multi-colored display of flowers that bordered the square.

It usually took forty-five minutes to get to the green market from her apartment following the same route she followed every week—across Tompkins Square Park which, as usual, was equally divided into overlapping areas: older people lounging and talking; junkies exchanging greetings and drugs; young people on the lawns sunning themselves; and chess tables which attracted serious players, people eating lunch, and a mix of both the homeless and those avoiding going home.

On the other side of the park, she continued her walk on Eleventh Street so she could look at the pastries that crowded the shelves of Veniero's, her favorite Italian bakery. Not because she was tempted to buy one, delicious as they looked, but because their arrangement pleased her, placed as she would have placed them, each tart or cake or pastry following the next by necessity of color and texture, order defying the chaos of need, as each shelf was carefully rearranged after being depleted of stock by frenetic customers.

After Veniero's, John's Restaurant was always her next stop. She loved to gauge how much the candle they displayed in their window had grown. The excess melted wax from the candles decorating each table was added to the huge mound of wax every night—and had been for more years than she could remember— as a testament to the longevity of the eatery and the loyal customers who ate there.

How long can all this last? she thought that day as she gazed at the candle burning in John's window like an eternal flame. She thought how food defined the blocks and those who lived in them. It was food that marked the boundaries as the old restaurants and eateries were slowly replaced by upscale, expensive restaurants that featured "fusion" menus that represented all ethnicities, and none. But it was getting late, and if she were to keep to her schedule, she would have to hurry.

She would buy a treat for herself from the vendor who stood at the entrance to the market, his glass case full of organic specialties—spinach empanadas with feta cheese and onions wrapped in thin whole wheat wafers, sweets made with tofu and rice syrup, all kinds of what were, for Rachel, exotic pleasures. She would listen to the roving musicians who filled the air with the sound of flutes from the Andes or guitar music reminiscent of the days when she had first moved to New York.

Rachel wondered if what attracted her to New York was the very thing most people complain about: the lack of space, the clutter, the noise. Rachel often wondered as she walked. Walking was her favorite time for wondering, for speculating about things she had read or heard in passing.

Do our experiences in the worlds of dream have as strong an impact on us as our waking experience, and if so what of the dreams we forget? That was one of Rachel's favorite wonderings. Probably because it was a puzzle that, by its very nature, could never be solved. And so, on this particular day, in the midst of her walking and wondering, tired and hot, Rachel, saw a baby carriage on sale in a bargain store window, and she bought it.

NINTH STREET TRIES TO GET A
WORD IN EDGEWISE

For the old a year is like a day, and a day like a year. That's the way old people measure time, and I am very old. You probably think this story is Rachel's creation, that it is her imagination, her memory at work. You wouldn't be entirely wrong, but you wouldn't be right either. After all, most of the events she remembers happened on me, or in the vicinity of me, and I have been here a lot longer than she has—hundreds of years, thousands, a millennia if you go back before I was partitioned into a street, to a time even my memory can no longer reach, when you and I were star dust, dark energy, dark matter. But today I am Ninth Street, and I am integrally entwined with the people who have lived on me in the past, who live on me now, who will live on me in the future, until that time when they are gone, and time runs backwards, and I become landscaped once again with trees and brooks (if there are any trees and brooks left). A time before humans took what was whole and separated it into squares and rectangles, streets and avenues.

Can you smell it, my past, as you walk my sidewalks? Can you smell the odor of silt after a November rain, the texture of moss beneath your feet so soft that the Lenape cannot be heard as they pass on their way to hunt or fish, or gather twigs for evening fires? Can you smell the rain before it became mixed with car fumes and smoke from burning refuse, or merged with the good sweet smell of fresh baked bread, a mélange of mixed odors: cigarette smoke, freshly washed laundry hanging on lines strung between back window sills, the aroma of Ukrainian, Caribbean, Puerto Rican, African American, Irish, Jewish cooking radiating from doors left open against the summer heat? Make no mistake, there was already the smell of decay before you arrived, of grass rotting under heavy rains, the occasional flood from a river not yet tamed, the sour odor of the bodies of animals decaying on their way to fertilizing new life.

In any case, whatever happens in the future, I will never be the same as I once was, because the history of each person who has lived on me has changed me, both as greatly and as subtly as the roots of the trees you have planted have cracked my sidewalks, the buildings you have constructed have first risen and then been demolished on my body.

In my present form, I am well over a hundred years old. Before that, I was part of a landscape of trees and streams that stretched from what is now Ave. A to the East River. Only the tiny rectangle called Tompkins Square Park remains of a farm that once was the great expanse of trees and hills and streams you now call Manhattan. But because you divided me, separated me, cut me off, tore out the grass and trees and shrubs, exiled the animals and plants that populated me, coated me with concrete, built houses on me, planted your trees after you had cut mine down, because you walked and rode on me, because you named me, I was brought into being. Ninth Street was born.

Do I mourn my previous lives before I was exiled from myself? That past is now vague, ambiguous, drowned in the chaotic footsteps that cross my sidewalks daily, in the noise of cars and bicycles, motorcycles, the buses that travel the avenues that border me. Sometimes I find it hard to breathe. The concrete that was poured over me leaves little room for air, even the small back gardens are mostly cemented over now, leaving only squares of earth enclosing the half dozen trees that line my block. I have been hollowed out underground to hide the maze of cables that provides you light and communication. Sometimes I feel like an overdressed diva, bedecked with ostentatious jewels, a victim of too much plastic surgery, who has become grotesque.

The amazing thing is even though in area I continue to get smaller until I am now only the one block, bounded by Avenues B and C, of a longer street that runs from the Hudson to the East River, I simultaneously seem to have grown larger from absorbing all the sights and sounds of the hundreds of thousands of people who have crossed me: the children rushing noisily every morning to grade school, lunch pails and mothers in hand; the Congo drums on Sunday morning echoing from the park as Cuban and Dominican and Puerto Rican women and men congregate to celebrate Elegua and Shango, Obatala and Yemaya, holding their heritage close to them through their songs and chants; the raucous sounds of jazz and rock mixing with a solitary flute played by an old African American man in a robe made of rainbow colors and sunlight. I have absorbed the lives of every man, woman, child, who has ever lived on me or crossed me on their way home, every sound I have ever heard, or vibration I have ever felt.

Sometimes it is all too much for me, blurring into a chaotic mass of feelings, sounds, colors, cavorting, swirling until they mesh into a color unlike any ever seen by your eyes, my senses being so different from yours, alien to the way you think and feel, because even though your senses are also mine, mine can never be yours.

I am not the first to say places retain part of the soul of those who inhabit them, but never has such a place had a chance to speak of it. And why me? Maybe because many writers, many artists have lived on me, because in their imagination, they brought me to consciousness. Perhaps it *is* Rachel's fault after all. With the magic that is her mind perhaps she conjured me into being. But regardless of the cause, my reason for speaking is quite simple: I want to be recognized. I demand to be recognized. I am as much a part of this story as any who exist because of me. Because of one building, 630 E. 9th Street, during one period of time, and no other.

Just remember that any street you walk, whether that street is aware of you or not, a piece of yourself is left irrevocably behind. You have become part of the memory of that place, and if others are sensitive, walking where you have walked, you will become part of them too. It could be as soft as a whisper, as sudden as a storm; it could be like a breeze, barely noticeable, or the sound of a building being demolished, or a ferocious fight

between friends or lovers or strangers. It could be a baby's cry, even a murder; the victim cut down, helpless, in the middle of the night. But whatever it is, the sum of all that street encompasses will become part of you, as you are absorbed, in turn, into it.

That's all I have to say. But maybe now when you walk on my block, you will sense me, a physical being, vibrating with life in all its variety, joy and pain.

A COLLECTOR, OF SORTS

Jerold had an unusual hobby. He collected people's faults. His collection was a compendium of mistakes, missteps, misinterpretations, miscommunications. Every fault he had ever experienced or observed was listed by time, date, category, individual. He loved Aristotle—the original cataloger, encyclopedist, sorter of particulars. He intended someday to publish an encyclopedia of his own. An *Encyclopedia of Foibles*, that's what he would call it. (*Foibles* being a gentler word than *faults*.) And everyone he had ever known or observed would be in it, including himself.

Jerald was proud of the fact he included himself in his project. How many others would have been as courageous? He made only one exception. Instead of mere pages, usually one or two at the most for everyone else, he kept a whole dossier of his faults. He added to it religiously every night before he went to sleep; and each morning after breakfast and a multi-vitamin to give him added endurance, he sat down at his tiny mahogany desk facing Ninth Street and carefully rehashed the events of the previous day, noting every time he had failed or faltered. He tried to avoid duplication, but that was impossible, some faults reappeared as soon as he thought he had corrected them. Sometimes in calmer—and perhaps saner?—moments, he wondered if he really wanted to correct them at all. If somewhere in the deepest recesses of his unconscious he wasn't proud of his failings, if he didn't feel that's what set him apart.

Here it must be noted that Jerald's failures, or foibles if you will, were not major, they were measured by quantity not quality. He had never committed a crime, never betrayed anyone; in fact, by any other standards but his own, he was quite a nice man, kind and considerate. But no one had ever constructed an encyclopedia out of one large indiscretion or misdeed; a novel perhaps, but not a catalog.

Jerald worked as a bookkeeper at Cooper Square, the local community housing council. The job was perfect for him. His cataloging of faults, as careful as he was, could sometimes be wrong, but numbers never failed him. If he made a mistake, even though it only amounted to a few cents, even though it might take hours to track it, he would search for it, pretending himself a great detective, or a defense attorney like Perry Mason, the lawyer in his favorite TV show, eliminating suspects until the real culprit finally emerged.

He lived happily among details and digits and schedules: the payroll that had to be met every Friday, the reports that had to be prepared for the monthly visit from the accountant. Accounts receivable, monthly expenditures, all were kept in neat columns in a slender leatherette journal; and when the office changed over to computers and electronic spreadsheets, he still held on to the pile of slim volumes, even though they were out of date and could safely be destroyed.

It was a good thing Jerald liked solitude, because he didn't have many friends. As soon as he made a new friend and they discovered his hobby, that was the end of their friendship. People don't want to have their faults collected, no matter how anonymously. Jerald had carefully coded names against numbers that only he could read, but even so his friends felt every time he looked at them, it was only because he wanted to see what they were doing wrong. He protested in vain that there was no judgment involved, just a cataloging, like a survey, but it was hopeless. So Jerald lived alone, trying most of his time to figure out how to connect with people who were putting an equal amount of time into figuring out how to avoid him.

For the life of him, Jerald couldn't understand what all the fuss was about. After all, he didn't mind listing his own faults, so why would anyone mind him listing theirs? He actually believed he was doing them a favor. As an objective observer, he felt they could learn a lot from his observations, that seeing their faults clearly would help them.

Then one day everything changed. Jerald fell in love.

He believed he had finally found the one person in the world with whom he could find no fault at all. Her name was Geraldine. Jerald and Geraldine, it was perfect! Geraldine also had a hobby. She collected people. The one talent she had was making people fall in love with her, both women and men. Her conquests defined her. So one after another, she acquired and discarded, acquired and discarded, being sure to keep souvenirs of each of her encounters. Her lovers, past and present, became acquisitions she looked on with pride, fully expecting them to do the same.

Geraldine was not consciously malicious or intentionally cruel, it was just that her own needs over-rode any other consideration. As her reputation became more public, she understandably found it harder to find new lovers, until one day she heard about a strange man named Jerald, whose hobby was collecting faults, and consequently how lonely he was. Instead of frightening her, his hobby intrigued her. At last Geraldine thought she had found someone who could truly appreciate her, because above all she wanted to be loved for who she was, with all her defeats, flaws, imperfections. Little did she know that to these, Jerald, the collector of faults, as a man in love, would be blind.

Geraldine was, at heart, a dreamer. Her mind was not filled with *what is* but rather with *what might be*. She delighted in the odors and textures of city life: the smell of coffee roasting in the morning, the noise of children playing stickball in the streets, the rowdiness of passersby returning from early morning revelries in bars and twenty-four hour coffee shops and restaurants.

She was enchanted by color: the palette of Tompkins Square Park, only a half block away, the trees' ubiquitous leaves dressed in their seasonal costumes, as winter branches sprouted pink and white buds, turning in Spring to predictable shades of green, then to autumn colors of orange and amber and red, to finally once again becoming barren branches decorated with icicles and snow piled perilously high. She delighted in the clothes of the children and their parents crossing through the park to get from one avenue to another as their colors closely matched the changing weather, growing darker in winter then gradually brighter as the days grew warmer, then fading to the somber tones of winter once again.

She loved the color of the snow as it transformed from pristine white to grey, even as it changed into the dirty brown slush left by the endless procession of boots and cars. She loved the silence of it, the way it muffled the everyday city noise, the din of cars and buses and cabs and the garbage trucks that passed in the middle of the night to pick up the cast offs of the day.

Geraldine had a recurring dream. She dreamt that she lived in an apartment on the edge of a large body of water—not the East River, even though that was only blocks away, and not the ocean in all its magnificence and glory. Her dream was not of a rustic home isolated in a landscape of grass and mountains and trees, it was of an apartment building just like the one she lived in, on an urban city block with old tenement structures sand-wiched side by side, their front windows facing the same dingy street as hers. The difference was the back door of her dream building opened onto the edge of a large lake, still and solemn, solitary and unaware of the creatures who lived in or around it, self-sufficient in the way she knew she could never be.

In her love of water she was very much like her neighbor Rachel, except unlike Rachel, Geraldine knew that her vision of water was a fantasy. One she could only live in the dark, at night, in the unconscious, which often seemed more real to her than her waking life.

Geraldine only really felt at peace standing in her door-way, the lake of her dreams stretched out before her—a lake she could look at, but never touch, that disappeared as soon as she opened her eyes, as much as she tried to keep its image in front of her. Often, trying to remember her dream, she would hear other people's voices fade until they echoed from a distance, like someone speaking a foreign language, how easily their words become unintelligible, meshing into one long indecipherable word.

"Are dreams the key? The ancient peoples thought so. The Mesopotamians believed they could communicate with their gods only through dreams and portents. Joseph escaped death because he could interpret the Pharaoh's dreams. Freud thought dream symbols hieroglyphs, the language of the unconscious, waiting to be deciphered."

Her question was directed toward Jerald, who was sitting across from her in their favorite outdoor café. Situated facing the park, it was a place Jerald particularly liked to come, drink his obligatory cup of coffee and "people watch" as he put it. It was a place where he could hone his powers of observation. He had to be careful though. New York was not a place where one wanted to be suspected of spying on one's neighbor, especially in the late Sixties, those days of increased paranoia, with so many in the area being involved in anti-war protests and political activity, and, in any case, staring too long at a stranger at any time, even under the best of circumstances, could provoke unpleasant consequences. Today, however, every bit of his attention was centered on the object of his affection, Geraldine.

"Why do you say that? Do you have any dream in particular in mind?" he responded hopefully, thinking how wonderful it would be if she were going to follow with a dream about him.

"Sometimes people say dreams are the eyes into the soul. But I have so much trouble remembering mine. Only special ones…"

"Yes, go on." A trembling Jerald could hardly contain himself.

"Why do you think I keep dreaming of an apartment whose back doors open onto a lake? Why I always need to feel its water so close to me."

What is *my* connection with water, Jerald puzzled, trying to find a way to connect with her dream world, a world that was so important to her. But try as he might, he could not find any way to weave himself into her dream, except by exclusion, the last prospect he wanted to entertain.

This relationship between Jerald and Geraldine had caused quite a stir in the neighborhood. Even in appearance they seemed to uniquely complement each other. Where Jerald was short and dark, Geraldine was tall and blond. He looked up to her and she looked down on him, which seemed entirely appropriate to those who knew them—as much as anyone could know two people most residents thought it best to avoid. When Geraldine had decided to move into Jerald's apartment on Ninth Street, their neighbors breathed a sight of relief. Maybe these two would neutralize each other and leave the rest of them in peace.

And for a time it seemed like that might indeed be the case. Jerald was fixated on his new found love, and Geraldine was intent on displaying as many faults as she could to him. In her own way, it was how she showed she cared for him. She left dirty dishes in the water, undercooked the meat and overcooked the vegetables—when she did cook, which was seldom—and never found a kind word or compliment for his cooking when he made her favorite foods. She twisted the toothpaste tube so viciously that after a couple of uses it was impossible to get any toothpaste out of it, she left hair in the shower and wet towels on the floor, and generally made a mess of everything. She blatantly flirted in front of him every chance she got and told him endless stories of past conquests.

You might say Jerald forgave her everything, but forgave is really the wrong word. He was in love, and love can find an excuse for any kind of aberrant behavior. He continued to write in his book religiously every morning. He continued to take voluminous notes every evening. And he was happy in his hobby, and Geraldine was happy in hers, having successfully made Jerald her latest and potentially most important acquisition. Because, you see, she never read his notebooks, she was so convinced that he delighted writing in them about her.

The only person in the building who had anything to do with them was Rachel. She couldn't care less whether Jerald wrote down her faults, it was totally immaterial to her, and besides, Jerald intrigued her, he appealed to her imagination. You wouldn't exactly call Rachel Jerald's friend, but at least she didn't try to avoid him at every opportunity. And so, through Rachel, Jerald began to discover the outside world.

At the time, the impact of the Vietnam War was slowly beginning to be felt in the neighborhood. Jerald was exempt from the draft, both because of his age and because physically he had at least three ailments that disqualified him, so for a long time he hadn't paid too much attention to what was going on in the larger world around him, occupied as he was by his dual obsessions, his journal of faults and his "faultless" love. But now, through conversations with Rachel, who was involved in community organizing and political protest, he began to add a paragraph each day to his daily journal entitled "Faults that Led Us into Vietnam."

Over time this paragraph became one page, then two pages, then a dozen, until he finally had to purchase a whole new binder to put them in. Little by little cataloging all the abuses of the war began to take up more of his energy and more space in his journals. As he continued to write about Vietnam, he began to note down other injustices, both on a national and local level, he had never noticed before, and as his journals began to change, his vision began to change as well. He remembered his mother describing the thin milky surface over her eyes that made it seem as if everything was lost in fog and, when it was finally removed, the shock of seeing things in focus again.

That's how he felt now, that he had never seen things in focus before. And slowly he became less interested in observing people's faults, and more in the interactions of the world around him. For over a dozen years, he had worked at a community housing council and been so preoccupied with numbers he had never really paid attention to what the numbers represented in people's lives: the tenants harassed by landlords trying to get them to leave as housing values in the neighborhood increased, people left homeless when the state mental hospitals were closed.

As soon as neighbors realized that his emphasis had shifted from chronicling their faults to recording the war and local issues, they stopped avoiding him, often sitting across from him in the park at one of the small tables usually occupied by men playing chess, where he liked to spend his time on sunny weekend days when Geraldine was at work at one of her temporary waitressing jobs. And sometimes even strangers would engage him in conversation if they had something in mind that they had read or seen on TV. Some tidbit of information they thought would be of interest to him.

Little did Jerald know that he would eventually become a well respected historian, an accurate and precise chronicler of events—of causes and effects. His appreciation of detail was invaluable. Unlike many other commentators, important in their own right, Jerald's accounting listed facts and numbers to the most minute detail: how many demonstrators were beaten by police in Chicago, by gender and race, age and occupation; an accounting of the casualties of the war on both sides (where the information was available) also categorized and if possible each person given a face as well as a name or number. If you wanted detailed, accurate information in those days before the Internet, Jerald was one of the sources you went to.

Geraldine, in the meantime, had still not read Jerald's journal, but it was obvious he was turning his attention more to the daily news, to hours of research at the St. Mark's Place library, to heated conversations with Rachel, so she became reconciled to the fact that he would not be exclusively devoted to her. She was more than willing to share her journal entries with the war and local activism, even to helping Jerald sift through the voluminous piles of information that were rapidly accumulating. She was still not aware not one single word in all of Jerald's work was devoted to her.

Then one evening, Geraldine's curiosity got the better of her. Jerald had gone with Rachel to a *Stop the Draft* meeting at the Metropolitan Church on West 4th Street, Geraldine pleading an upset stomach from overindulging at a local Indian restaurant the night before. By now, Jerald's "encyclopedia" had grown to more than a dozen large volumes, pristine pages gathered together in large black spring binders—precisely annotated and indexed.

With more excitement than she had felt in years, exactly as if approaching a new love, she tremulously reached for the first volume and then the second, the third, and then more rapidly the fourth, the fifth.

Anticipation turned to dread as one by one the volumes fell to the floor, page after page of neighbors, of passersby, then the volumes about the war, local and national and international politics, but nothing about her. She finally came to the last volume dated July 1, 1974.

There was nothing with her name on it, or in it.

Then it struck her, maybe she had a volume all her own! But search as she might, she couldn't find it. Perhaps he had hidden it. Of course, that was it! He had hidden her journal of faults because he was afraid of her reaction if she saw it. That *must* be it! Breathing a sight of relief, she decided when he came home, she would ask him to see her volume, reassuring him that she would not be hurt, it would be helpful to her, she would be grateful to him.

Geraldine could hardly wait. She decided she would fix his favorite meal of fried chicken, mashed potatoes, peas, and Rocky Road ice cream. For one night she would not exhibit an inventory of faults for him to admire. For one night she would be as "faultless" as she could, in honor of this special occasion.

When Jerald arrived home, he was grumpy and tired. Everything had seemed to conspire to irritate him. It had been a long stressful day at work, the meeting had turned out to be one of those tedious affairs whose main purpose seemed to be to set another series of meetings, and to top it off, Rachel had volunteered him to provide lists of wounded soldiers and statistics on conscientious objectors, and it all had to be done immediately, for an emergency *ad hoc* rally that had been called for the following weekend.

Imagine his surprise when he saw Geraldine waiting for him in her best outfit in a spotless apartment smelling of his favorite foods. At first he was puzzled, and then it slowly began to dawn on him that maybe, just maybe, what he had taken as inconsequential habits, a quirkiness on Geraldine's part—her inability to cook, clean up after herself, the cruelty which he chalked up to ignorance, carelessness, naiveté—were all intentional. But *why*? It was all too much. He was so tired, he couldn't think. He just wanted to go to bed, sleep it off, like he would after a bad night out and too much to drink. He would wake up with a headache, but with everything normal again. But tonight he had work to do.

Geraldine could sense something was wrong and decided to flat out ask him where the volume was that was dedicated to her faults.

"Jerald, dear," coaxing, pleading. "Where is it?"

"Where is what?"

"You know, the volume devoted to me. The volume of my faults."

"What volume?"

Was he so dense he couldn't understand her question? Was he still hiding, afraid of what she might say or do?

"Don't worry. I won't be angry. To the contrary, it will help me to see my flaws. To correct them...for you. I do want to see what you've written about me. Please. I won't be hurt. Please. I promise."

He stared at her in disbelief. Why would she think he had written about her? And secretly at that? Something he would never think of doing.

"But I haven't written anything about you."

"Nothing?"

"Nothing. Why would I?"

"But I have so many faults."

"Even if that were so, I would never write them down. I love you."

Geraldine was stunned into silence. Jerald mumbled an excuse and took off to the small room he had set aside for his work, a place that had always before made him feel at peace. He sat and poured over his notes and the information he had gathered in his journals. But even they seemed foreign to him now, his meticulous sense of order torn apart. Geraldine threw their uneaten food in the trash and fled to their bedroom, leaving a mess behind. This time, it was unintentional.

In the morning Jerald left for work before Geraldine was up, leaving a note that he expected to be home late—he had a meeting after work and would stay and do the week's payroll. When he finally did come home, he pretended nothing had happened and hoped Geraldine would do the same.

Habits are hard to break, and even though Jerald was now concentrating entirely on events in the outside world and had made a number of new friends, he was still at heart a collector, of sorts. As for Geraldine, she realized after a few short weeks that it was time for her to move on to her next acquisition. Even if nothing would ever satisfy her completely, maybe tonight would be the night her dream would return, and she would live once more secure in a tiny apartment perched on the edge of a boundless, if ephemeral body of water, her beloved lake.

MIRROR, MIRROR

Rachel had lived in her third floor rear apartment fronting the courtyard for over twenty years when she finally decided to look into the small round sterling silver mirror her mother had given her on her sixteenth birthday, a mirror she had in turn given to Norma, the woman she considered at the time "The One"—a name she subsequently gave to everyone she fell in love with. "The One" lasted five years before she moved on, and in parting left the mirror behind, along with several other items she no longer had any use for, which included a heart-broken Rachel.

When Rachel originally received her "sweet sixteen" gift, she barely looked at it, much less into it. She threw it into a bottom dresser drawer where it kept company with her collection of mismatched socks. She was disgusted that once again her mother had given her a present that pleased her rather than one that would please Rachel, who would have welcomed books or records as a first choice, but definitely not "Little Lady" bath powder or the other sundries popular as gifts for young women at the time, and certainly not a mirror with a sterling silver frame. For one thing, it looked suspiciously like a gift her mother might have received— everyone knew how much her mother liked to look at herself— and, already having many elaborate and expensive mirrors, passed on to her daughter.

Rachel liked gifts you could touch, gifts that were carefully chosen, that brought you close to the person who gave them to you. Gifts like that were even better than photographs to remember the giver by. More than just the literal rendering of a person's face or features, they were a tangible reminder that someone cared about you. For that reason, Rachel always kept her gifts, even when they were no longer of any use: a tin with mountains and rivers in high relief left over from a gift of exotic teas; a piece of colored ribbon, red or green or silver or stripped in yellow and purple, from a gift of food or candy; a dark blue sweater with gleaming white snowflakes and two reindeer with crystal eyes, long out of fashion and worn thin from use; a lace handkerchief with her initials on it—she had a collection of these, along with a stack of scarves she would never wear, but would never give away. The silver mirror, however, she left at home when she went away to college and afterward moved across a continent to work in New York City and live on East Ninth Street, a half block from Tompkins Square Park.

On her twenty-fifth birthday, much to her surprise—she hadn't received a gift from her parents in years, a phone call acknowledging her birthday was the most she could hope for—she received a large box from home. She eagerly opened it, only to find what was left of her childhood belongings with the excuse her mother had come across them cleaning house, had gathered them together and decided to send them to her. What her mother considered of any real value she had given away: a prized stamp collection to the postman for his son, a collection of tiny porcelain horses to a friend's child who admired them. Rachel, in a fit of rage, stuffed the box in back of some old clothes on the top shelf of her closet, feeling as if the last remnants of her presence had been swept up, discarded like unwelcome trash.

After many abortive relationships with men during the heady days of the so-called "sexual revolution," relationships that left her feeling lonely and used, the first time she and Norma touched, Rachel knew she had finally experienced love in its fullest sense, the coming together of sexual pleasure and emotional longing. In this woman, in her body, in the way she moved and spoke and thought, Rachel felt at peace. Not a peace without problems or pain, not a fantasy peace, the peace of knowing she was in the right place, she was no longer lost.

When Norma came to live with her a year later, cleaning the apartment to make space, they came upon the box still resting unopened. Norma, out of a curiosity that Rachel didn't share, insisted on seeing what was in it. Nestled among the various bits and pieces of assorted junk Rachel immediately threw away, there were things she had loved as a small child and decided to keep: a battered yellow cloth dog, one ear missing, with large black spots for eyes; a stiff wooden Pinocchio, almost two feet long, with limbs that still moved, that she had slept with at night to protect her from bad dreams and left her in the morning bruised, but happy; a white woolen donkey with a bright red mouth and a music box inside that played "Home on the Range"; her baby shoes coated in bronze; and at the bottom of the box, the small silver mirror. Since Norma seemed fascinated with it, Rachel gave it to her. When Norma left, she left the mirror behind.

Intending to throw it away as a reminder of yet another failed relationship, Rachel, as if by accident, looked into it. To her surprise, what was reflected in it was not the face that was familiar to her, was not her image as she knew it from the antique mirror in her living room, from photographs, from her own imagination. Granted it resembled her, but there was something alien about it. It was as if she were looking simultaneously at a complete stranger and at someone more familiar to her than any image of herself she had ever seen. It was not a feeling like a dream or a nightmare, not the visual distortion you might see on drugs, or a hallucination that would seem at odds with reality. What was inside the silver frame was the only thing that seemed real. The cold metal feel of it invaded her psych, held her, bound her. Even though looking in the mirror frightened her, the familiarity of it was something she could not deny or evade. She found herself whispering to it, compulsively pouring out her heart to it—not to her reflection in the mirror, but to the mirror itself, as if the silvered glass that held her reflection had a life of its own. Was it a living, breathing entity like the infamous mirror in Snow White? Would it hear her and respond in the only way it knew how, by absorbing her and distorting her image in unimaginable ways?

"If I had looked in you when I was sixteen what would I have seen? Why is my face lost in you now? Where have you hidden me?"

Rachel clutched the mirror as if she could squeeze answers from it, as if the cold silver frame could magically transform into something organic, that would respond to her with warmth and fluidity and not the heaviness of metal. She couldn't remember when she had ever felt so cold. But this frost came from deep within her, burning as only ice can burn, scalding her from inside.

"Norma, my love, when we were together, when you owned this mirror, the only image I had of myself was what I saw reflected in your eyes. Is that what I see in my mirror now? The mirror you so coveted and won from me. If only, like Alice, I could walk through this looking-glass, maybe I could find myself on the other side, or like Cocteau's Orpheus drown in molten glass. Maybe I already am on the other side, caught in a reality where everything is reversed and nothing makes sense."

"When I looked at myself through your eyes, I saw you. Yes, that sums it up nicely. That is exactly right. Was that the reason you left me? But what does it matter? We parted, separated, said 'goodbye,' tried to be friends, failed even at that. Not that you said anything to me directly. You didn't have to. It was there, in your face, the way you spoke of other women, other men, with that longing in your voice."

But that was so long ago. Another life.

Taking a marker from her desk drawer, Rachel drew an outline around the image of her face, then meticulously drew in her eyes, her nose, leaving her mouth blank, a face without a voice. Another lie. Another irony. Not a face without a voice, a voice without a face. Watching television, listening to the radio, reading comic books and movie magazines, even the classics; listening to all the myths and lies, sensing her parents hopes and dreams, what they wanted, what they would have liked her to be or not to be. All this was contained in that one small mirror. That stranger's face that stared back at her, mocking her, twisting her name into something unrecognizable.

She realized she had spent five years with a woman who never saw her. And because of this she had ceased to see herself. The day after Norma left and Rachel finally looked at herself in the small silver mirror her mother had given her so many years before, she threw it against the wall, watching it break into pieces, not caring about the seven years of bad luck that might follow, years she felt she already had behind her. But unable to let go completely she had gathered the pieces up one by one, and one by one had thrown them into the trash, until finally all that was left was a broken frame that still had one large piece tenaciously clinging to it.

And it was this one piece that she was staring into now, and it was on this one piece she saw Norma's face reflected back at her, splintered, broken, but in her mind, still whole.

THE SECRET HEARTS OF CLOCKS

Orange changes luck, and Laura desperately needed her luck to change. Orange is the color of success, energy, attraction. These were qualities she secretly felt she lacked and consequently looked for in other people. Orange was the last color she would have chosen to wear or to decorate her home. She would never have bought an orange pillow or an orange rug or an orange shirt, but every night she burned an orange candle and prayed for change.

On Seventh Street, four buildings east of the Polish Catholic Church, *Other Worldly Waxes* nestled between two apartment complexes, its windows lined with candles of every description and hue, some in elaborate holders, others in tall glass containers. Two of the candles, devoted to the Yoruba orishas Elegua and Yemaya, were intricately carved. The blessing candle for Elegua, guardian of the crossroads, was red with superimposed rows of black and silver triangles; the candle for Yamaya, queen of the waters, was blue emblazoned with silver and white.

Each time Laura passed the candle shop, she stopped to inspect the windows before going in to purchase her monthly ration of hope. Laura was an actress. What she lacked in talent, she made up in determination. Laura pursued older men, not because they reminded her of her father, or because of any other popular psychological conundrum, but because she believed they were the only people who needed her more than she needed them. Her current lover, Alberto Rodriguez, a classical guitarist and folksinger from Chile, was twenty-five years her senior.

Unlike Laura, Alberto had talent, even a touch of genius. His playing was unique. He might have made a name for himself, done great things, if he weren't constantly losing focus. Sometimes in the early morning when it was still dark, he would awaken suddenly, convinced he was back in his birthplace, Santiago. Directly in front of him, he imagined the worn oak door of the bedroom where he had spent his childhood, the blue painted walls, the poster of Violeta Parra tacked up for inspiration next to the hand-drawn sketch of his hero Salvador Allende. Both images were left behind when he fled Chile in the summer of 1973, anticipating the disaster that was to follow two months later.

September 11, 1973: the day of the military coup, the death of Allende, the internment of many of his closest friends. September 11, 1973: the day Alberto Rodriguez lost his past and, he feared, his future as well.

Every night, faithfully, Alberto would read aloud a poem of Pablo Neruda or Gabriela Mistral and play the melodies of Violeta Parra and his other idol, Victor Jara, one of the many who had died at the hands of Pinochet and his cohorts. Blending his voice with theirs, Alberto heard once again the music of the peñas, the gathering places where he first learned the guitar and the music that now gave him his only true solace. He often accompanied himself on an old-fashioned charango, a stringed instrument with an armadillo shell back. The sole instrument he was able to rescue from Chile, it hung on his wall where he could always see it, when it was not cradled lovingly in his arms.

Alberto had memorized almost every line of his favorite poem of Neruda's, "To Don Asterio Alarcón, Clocksmith of Valparaíso." Reciting it aloud conjured up for him the Chile that survived now only in his mind. Even though it was not the Valparaíso of the poem, with its "streets of sea and wind..." he remembered best, it was the Santiago of his boyhood—the smell of wine on the early morning breeze, the Andes in the distance covered with snow, the cool ease of the city and its people.

Alberto imagined himself Don Asterio, living that most orderly of lives as a fixer of clocks, surrounded by the linear melody of their steady, unfaltering beat. He saw himself hunched over his worktable *(inmovilizado)* "motionless," like the clock smith, magnifying glass attached to his forehead by an old black elastic band—his spyglass into the soul—as he peered into *(el enigma)* "the mystery," "the secret hearts of clocks."

Sometimes, Alberto liked to mix lines of his favorite poems like improvisations on a musical theme, savoring each word in Spanish as it filled the cavities of his mouth and heart.

Alberto had a dream once about a clock. A very peculiar clock. Larger than him by half a head or more, its ticking was magnified to an almost unbearable pitch. In the dream, as the clock beat its percussive rhythm, its huge second hand circled with relentless precision. As he stared at it, the second hand slowed until it stopped and he was drawn toward it, and into it, between the seconds of time, and there, in the silence of the timeless which was not silence, but one prolonged, barely discernible tone, he slid into a world of color and light and indescribable beauty until he woke, his head aching with loss.

How different it was from his everyday world where he occupied the apartment under Rachel on the second floor of the small back building. Where each morning he watched people on their way to work throw out their garbage in the adjacent back yard and visualized his image embossed on the glossy plastic bags: sandwich-size Albertos, kitchen-size Albertos; jumbo-trash-can-size Albertos. All on their inevitable voyage into final exile.

Alberto made the small salary he needed to survive by giving music lessons and an occasional concert. Money didn't matter to him. His students served a much more important function. Alberto needed them to validate the persona he projected as "el maestro," even though he was well aware he was cheating them of the true source of the powerful music he produced, the wellspring of his passion, by hiding the complexity of contradictions that was the real Alberto Rodriguez.

When Alberto had first met Laura he had no idea that she was attracted to him. He was playing a concert at the public library on 10th Street. He so seldom had an opportunity to try out new songs and the audience at the weekly series devoted to showcasing local "talent" was small but appreciative. Laura had stopped by that night on her way home from buying her monthly supply of candles and was immediately taken by Alberto and his music. There was a sense of isolation about him that appealed to her, of something that would be always just out of reach. She knew the moment she saw him she had found her match.

Alberto, for his part, couldn't believe his luck, that this beautiful young woman found him attractive and appreciated his music. It was more than he ever expected could happen in this strange new world in which he reluctantly found himself ensconced.

Laura devised an exquisite torture for her troubadour lover. It came under the heading of what she called her "improvisations." Using the excuse she was an actress and needed the practice, she would create scenarios which she would then present to Alberto, as her "only available partner," to act out with her. They were scenes of enormous but subtle degradation that, naturally, required an audience.

When he objected she would cajole a reluctant Alberto: "What good is an actress without an audience? When you play your guitar, you have an audience. You need an audience. Why am I different? Do you think I need an audience less than you?"

It was a hard argument to counter.

Laura had also devised a most ingenious form of rehearsal. Her basic story lines were constructed in bed. Alberto, the musician, liked to listen more than talk. Laura, the actress, liked to talk more than listen. That might have made for a perfect pairing except, under these circumstances of delicate love, Alberto found Laura's incessant chatter annoying, and she found his silence infuriating.

When they first met, they stayed in bed for hours on end, happy to be lying in each other's arms experiencing the touch of a hand, the fold of a lip, the way their bodies smelled, slick and warm. They were both experienced in the techniques of passion; but barely a month into their relationship, Laura began making up playlets to stimulate her desire.

As the weeks dragged on, the scenes Laura constructed became progressively more complex. Her imagination strayed from tales of sexual pleasure toward stories of desire, frustration, and rage until even in the act of making love, they scarcely touched.

Laura always made sure that her dramas included a scene that featured Alberto's music, that gave him a chance to share his obsession with all things Chilean. It was a velvet snare. She knew if there was any chance he might finally turn away from her, he would never relinquish the opportunity to celebrate his homeland and, not incidentally, his virtuosity, with a willing audience.

So her scripts always started with a flirtation, an appreciation, a seduction, before they drifted into imagined wrongs, recriminations, violations of trust, and degenerated from there into betrayal, righteous indignation, rage. Whatever the specific details, the plot was always the same, and it was always Alberto who was revealed as the villain.

One night Laura blundered.

Alberto might accept or ignore whatever insults, subtle or direct, she offered him, but the one thing he would not tolerate was any insult to the heroes of his imagination and wonder. The evening in question, Laura had concocted a story about a repairer of watches, a tender of time, a clocksmith, based on Alberto's cherished Don Asterio. For weeks, she had felt Alberto gradually losing interest in their relationship, and although his departure was what she, consciously or unconsciously, most desired, she wanted it to be her decision, not his.

She had practiced it in bed with predictable results. Whispering in his ear the outline of the plot, she stroked his arms, his chest, his thighs, caressing him between his legs until he was firm, and she could tell he was barely breathing. She kept up a running dialogue between caresses, between lingering kisses, now tracing his body with her tongue as she paused at exactly the right moments to relate his part in the upcoming panorama, making him groan with desire as she edged nearer and nearer his crotch with her tongue as she stopped once again to whisper her plans and his place in them, knowing he was paying little attention to her words.

But the following week, during the public performance of this, her latest masterpiece, she went too far. In her new improvisation she had ingeniously cast herself as the watchsmith, and Alberto as the watch. They had invited a small group of friends, six in all, for dinner and the performance. She called her drama, "Cities of the Sea." While it was loosely based on the Neruda poem, the story and the words that went with it were hers.

In honor of this special evening, Alberto would play his own music. He had composed a suite of songs without lyrics. As he strummed the guitar and then the charango, he hummed the sounds of the ocean waves as they broke against the piers of Valparaíso and Viña del Mar, of Isla Negra, of the long narrow coast of Chile, that thin cylinder of land bordered by mountains and sea. He quickly lost himself in the music, so like the sound in his dream of time suspended, a place beyond moments and memory.

And into that rapture, into the profundity of his mediation, came the impossible, the unforgivable, Laura's voice, her incessant chatter, even as the night before, his body lifted toward hers in love, as she lay on top of him, pushing against him, as he turned and flung himself against her, as if to free himself, he became more entangled in her, until finally drained, he surrendered, and lying spent in her arms, gave up his will in their mutual embrace.

But this night he was playing the melody of his deepest desire, and her voice was an inexcusable interruption, a hurricane, a cacophony of wind of rain descending in all its fury, and he began to roar, to bellow like an animal, to scream and cry, swinging his instrument at her in rage.

He realized too late his sublime moment of retaliation, his long-awaited triumph, had been part of her unwritten script all along. Acknowledging the enormity of his defeat, he quietly apologized to her and to their guests, and placing his guitar like an offering at her feet, he surrendered once more.

He couldn't recount how many times friends had lectured him about his deprecating, self-destructive behavior. He didn't disagree with them. He knew everything they said was true. He wasn't ungrateful for their support. He depended on it. What they didn't understand was that he, Alberto Rodriguez, was truly a man possessed. Not by a woman. The foundation of his love for Laura, the reason he dreaded the day he would lose her, was that Laura had done what no one else had ever done for him. She had given him the ultimate gift: the gift of regret.

So he forgave her everything: her selfishness, her arrogance, her conceit. If Laura was not conscious of the role she played in his life, all the better. He could hide the truth deep within himself, undisturbed, in the "the secret heart" of Alberto Rodriguez.

He felt that he, like Don Asterio was *(detenido en el tiempo)* "trapped in the flow of time." But unlike Don Asterio, it was not a pact he had either searched out or agreed to; it was a contract he had been forced to sign.

Alberto had a photograph of a statue of the Buddhist monk Hoshi pinned on the wall next to his charango. Hoshi, perfectly calm, in deep meditation, his face torn open, his inner face an exact duplicate of the face he showed to the world.

So unlike me, Alberto thought, or Laura, the two of us always onstage, posturing for each other, revealing nothing, providing each other with a world in which we can remain as we are: stubborn, intransigent, saying one thing, meaning another, constantly circling each other waiting for an opening, secretly praying it will never come.

And so it continued, until one unusually hot morning in early fall which had everyone remarking that indeed there might be such a phenomenon as global warming.

The sun bright, the streets almost empty of pedestrians, Laura, on her way home, weary from another questionable night with Alberto, stopped once again in front of the mysterious candle shop. Even darkened, with an steel grate protecting the precious treasures inside, it retained its fascination for her.

Three blocks away, Alberto walked over to the TV and turned off the morning news. Each year on this date he performed the same ritual. In absolute silence, sitting in the brown leather chair facing his front window, he wrote down his most secret thoughts, marking in his memory another anniversary of the end of his world.

It was twenty-nine years since the violent overthrow of the Allende government and the installation of the military regime;

twenty-nine years since Alberto had left Chile for the safety of New York. Even though Pinochet was deposed in 1990 and there was no longer any reason Alberto could not return to Chile, New York was now his home. New York had become for him a purgatory in which he had found his own special brand of peace.

That bright fall morning, the 11th of September, 2001, his window open to the sun, when Alberto finished writing his reflections, in honor of his favorite poem and in strict accordance with the procedure he had faithfully practiced for the last twenty-nine years, he carefully printed at the top of the page, "The Secret Hearts of Alberto Rodriguez," and at the bottom, precisely at 8:30AM, directly below his signature, the time and date of his latest meditation

MR. GROAN

Paul sat very still, inhaling, exhaling, holding his breath in, drawing it out. He saw himself balancing on it as it became longer and thinner, until it became invisible, stretching through space. When he finally got up, after what could have been hours, his muscles tight with the effort of negotiating the distances he had traveled, he looked longingly at his watch. How much time had he saved today? How many minutes had he stored away?

But maybe he should be moving faster not slower, rushing, not withdrawing. Einstein proved the faster you move, the more time slows, at least as you approach the speed of light. Even at his fastest, he was not nearly that fast! Besides which he was firmly planted on earth, not hurling through the dark vacuum of space. Not lost, like Rachel, in the heavens.

No, he was "down to earth," a realist, grounded.

Grounded—what a peculiar word. Steady, sure, secure, stable—all the "*s*" words people admire. But for Paul the word *grounded* always brought to mind, when he heard it, the stern (another *s* word) face of this father towering above him. He could see his father's lips, huge, moving in slow motion (a slowness he wished he could mimic) forming the dreaded words: "*Y o u a r e G R O U N D E D.*" Meaning he was a prisoner, meaning he was caged, trapped, *un*steady, *un*sure, *in*secure, *un*stable. A strange word: *grounded.*

A word he had pursued and avoided all his life.

Paul had grown up on a small farm in Iowa, surrounded by acres of cornfields, oats and hay and food that was as white and pale as the faces of his brothers and sisters, all five of them, during the long months when winter reached so far inside him, he carried it even to this day.

His father was a stoic man who felt that his love, or at least his duty to his family, was adequately represented by the food he placed on their table each day: creamed corn, scalloped potatoes, cream of mushroom soup, milk, bread so white that even when toasted the white shone through, bread pudding, chicken a lá king, and Paul's favorite, banana cream pie.

As a teenager Paul, the youngest sibling, was constantly in trouble. All he could think of was how he could get out of the milky prison that was his childhood. It was the mid 1950s and exciting tales of rebellion filtered in through movies, newspapers, and magazines, stirring his adolescent imagination. He began to wear his jeans tight, low and rolled up at the bottom like James Dean in "Rebel Without a Cause." He longed for an orange leather jacket like Dean's or perhaps a black leather motorcycle jacket like Marlon Brando's in "The Wild Ones"—the accoutrements of the true individualist.

Paul tried to see in his own family glimpses of the sadistic father and domineering mother of "Rebel…" But even he had to admit his father was strict and distant, but he was hardly sadistic, and Paul's mother only wanted to make sure her family unit functioned as orderly as the accounts she kept so carefully in her small precise handwriting in a diary that never left her side.

The struggle for a farmer to survive is constant, but Paul's family wasn't poor. Even though their farm was small measured against the mega-farms of agribusiness, Paul could walk for hours between the rows of corn or grain imagining himself reaching the end of his family's land and entering the great world outside.

One difficulty presented itself to him immediately upon entering his senior year in high school. Unlike the heroes in the movies he wished to emulate, Paul had to decide what he was going to do with his life, specifically how he was going to make a living. He had always spent his summers working on the family farm, but unless he wanted that occupation to extend as far into the future as the endless acres he had thus far tried so futilely to escape, he had to decide what to do, and quickly.

He told his parents he would follow his three older brothers to college—his sister, Kate, had married immediately after graduating high school, much to his parents' disgust, and had already begun her family with not one, but two children. Her first child was delivered a little short of nine months after the wedding, fueling all kinds of rumors. The truth was Kate, being an exemplary "good girl" of the fifties, remained a virgin until her wedding night.

It was his parents' dream, unlike Paul's, that all of their children finish college. Two of the brothers had already decided to pursue graduate work in agriculture and return to the farm that was, and would always be, their home. The brothers loved the farm with its acre upon acre of rich soil and growing things. They loved the yellow and cream colors of the corn cradled by rich green cushions as it reached maturity, leaves bending to touch the ground. They even loved the dry straw-colored mat that was left scattered on the soil after the corn was harvested.

But Paul was tired of vast spaces and the emptiness they created inside him. He longed for urban dirt and city noise. He yearned for closeness and crowding. When his father demanded once again to know what he would do when he graduated, Paul said he would, yes, continue on to Iowa State University and major in agricultural management, much to his father's astonishment and delight.

That was his declared intention. Undeclared was his private ambition to leave and go as far away as he could from everything he had ever known. There was nothing around him that fired his imagination—not land, not family, not friends, not even the young woman he had briefly fallen in love with his senior year. The shock of thinking he had made her pregnant, and the greater relief of finding out he hadn't, was the last defining piece that sent him in the direction of Iowa State, and beyond. Because instead of getting off the bus at the place indicated on his ticket and finding transportation to the dorm room that awaited him, Paul immediately bought another ticket to the destination he had intended all along—New York City.

Now approaching forty, he felt time slipping away from him. He had not found whatever it was he had fled from, or toward. He had wandered from one job, one location in the city, to another, as the years slid by beneath him, barely noticed, until one day he no longer recognized the young man who had boarded a bus bound for one place and had wound up in another.

His escape, perhaps because it was so rapid, was only partial. He was still haunted by dreams patterned in white and yellow, faint outlines that dimmed in and out of focus like the patterns of waving corn stalks from his youth. Often he awoke troubled, uncertain of who or where he was.

As much as Paul considered Rachel unrealistic, a person who lived in her dreams, rather than acting them out in the real world, as he felt he did, she was the one person he most often chose to spend time with. They would sit on the roof for hours, talking, watching the stars, or, on most nights, watching the places where the stars would be if they could be seen through the haze caused by cloud cover and the reflection of city lights and noise.

Paul was known by the neighborhood kids as "Mr. Groan." Instead of taking it as the insult it was intended to be, it was a title he took as a compliment. He had complaining down to a science. He felt complaining was good for the soul. Letting out everyday frustrations and injustices harmlessly to the willing ears of his friend and whoever else would listen. What was the point of suffering in silence? What was the point of being a good sport, a good fellow, someone who didn't make trouble, who took whatever life dealt out and never let it show?

"How hard," he would repeat over and again to Rachel. "How very hard it would be to pretend it doesn't matter, to pretend I don't care."

What could Rachel reply to a question that had no answer? That wasn't really a question, but a statement of fact, a summary of a lifetime spent, as far as Paul was concerned, with very little in the way of recompense. The problem was Paul's soliloquies made Rachel feel overlooked, like neither she nor her opinion mattered. But she knew better than to say anything, her job was to listen.

It seemed like it was always her job to listen.

"You're such a good listener," Paul would say. "It's a pleasure talking to you."

Rachel would answer, as usual, with silence.

One night, however, Paul surprised her. Rachel sat, waiting to listen, but Paul also sat as if he too were listening, or for once had run out of things to say.

Rachel waited quietly. Finally, after an hour or more had gone by, she could bear it no longer.

"Paul?"

He turned slowly, looking at her as if he had been waiting patiently all evening for her to speak.

"Paul, is anything wrong?"

He sat, watching—yes, watching—the words as they slipped from her mouth. One syllable soft, the next round and hard, the next spiked and sharp. *Any*—all soft and drawn out, bouncing slowly, each bounce lower and closer to the scarred asphalt roofing. He listened carefully, afraid the word might not reach him at all.

Nnnnnnnnkneeee. He repeated the word aloud, *Nnnnnnnnkneeeee.* A nice sound, like sand before wind. How like Rachel to say words that were so close to water. Then *thing*, spiked and sharp.

During that conversation, if you could call it a conversation, the thought occurred to Paul that Rachel had more to teach him than he had been prepared to learn. Not with words, she said so little, with her presence, her demeanor. Through all the years he had known her, she scarcely seemed to have changed. It was as if she remained still while things around her grew old.

Now he understood. It was her stillness that kept time at bay. Rachel could teach him this one great lesson. How to keep still. So the two of them would sit for hours, Paul playing the eager student, mimicking Rachel's every movement, her every breath.

It was inevitable Rachel would one day get bored and, feeling Paul had found her unworthy, cease her visits altogether. Paul, on the other hand, was perfectly content. He was grateful to Rachel. Through Rachel he had learned to thwart his, and her, greatest enemy—time.

PASSION & PEACE

Passion and Peace were sisters. They looked so much alike some people mistook them for twins, even though two years separated them almost to the day. They had lived in the building on Ninth Street so long they couldn't remember when they had moved in. Maybe they had been born there. Nobody knew or cared for that matter, especially not them. They didn't even care enough to ask their parents, who were still alive and in charge of all their faculties, including the talent of remembering.

Passion and Peace (or PP as they came to be known by giggling neighbors when they were together, and they were rarely apart) shared duties tending the small grocery store halfway down the block. They worked six hours a day, six days a week. Even their work schedule preserved symmetry. Every Sunday, their one day of rest, the-twins-who-weren't headed west to the Ukrainian Eastern Orthodox Church on Seventh Street between Second and Third Avenues.

Passion and Peace were odd names at best, but certainly so for two traditional Ukrainian women. Nobody seemed to know who had chosen their names. Their parents were no help, probably not wanting to confess to youthful indiscretions, whether in behavior or the art of choosing proper names. However, theirs weren't the only strange names in the neighborhood that originated from fine, upstanding families. The Eighteenth Century graveyard on Second Street to this day still proudly proclaims its indebtedness to one Preserved Fish, a prominent merchant and descendant of a famous ancestor, Hamilton Fish, the sixteenth governor of New York. Next to that, what were a couple of innocuous girls' names like Passion and Peace?

It was logical to assume they had been named as babies with the appellate that described them best: Passion, naughty and dramatic; Peace, quiet and loving. Nothing could have been further from the truth. Passion, unlike her sister, was loving almost to a fault and trusted everyone. She made the all-too-human mistake of generalizing to the world from herself and couldn't comprehend that anyone would lie to her or cheat on her. Peace, on the other hand, trusted no one. Her community of friends consisted almost exclusively of old lovers. She trusted people only insofar as she could control them. And who can be controlled better than someone who still loves you but you no longer love?

While Passion longed for nothing more than the end of a long work day when she could finally go home, put up her feet and rest, Peace made so many dates she often forgot who she was going out with; and since she felt that a big piece of her was missing without her sister, she rarely failed to drag her along. If there was one person in the world Peace depended on being there for her, it was her sister, and by every indication that would never change.

Which was all well and good until Passion announced to her shocked sister one very cold day in late November, three hours before their annual Thanksgiving feast was to begin, that she was in love and intended to get married before the year was out.

It seems that Passion had been seeing one of her customers, a quiet man named Ben, who found Passion's calm manner irresistible. He had gained ten pounds a month for four months running, daily buying large slices of seven-layer cake, the only food in the store he could tolerate, and decided the only way to put a brake on his newly acquired girth was to ask her to marry him.

"What do you mean you're getting married? Whoever to?"

"His name is Ben. He's been coming to the store every day for months. Last week he asked me out for a cup of coffee. He took me to a nice place, you know that little coffee shop on Tenth Street across from the park, and we talked a lot and stayed on for dinner."

"Well, so…?"

"And yesterday he came into the store as usual, but instead of buying anything, he asked me to marry him."

"And…?"

"And I accepted."

"*Just like that?*"

"Just like that."

Peace stood for once beyond words, her ubiquitous cigarette forgotten in the crystal ashtray a former boyfriend had given her the Christmas before, dumbfounded by the action her mild-mannered sister had taken that not even she, with all her bravado, would have dared.

"*But you don't know him!*"

"I know him well enough. He's a gentle man and good looking too, in his way. I want to get married. I want my own home."

"This *is* your home. *Here. With me.*"

Peace could feel her face flaming up, as it was wont to do when she got mad, suddenly, with no warning. At the same time, her cigarette was beginning to burn down, saturating the air with the noxious fumes filters emanate when they catch fire. She paused for a moment to crush it out, grinding it in a circle in the ashtray. She tried to gather her thoughts, calm down, surprised herself at the strength of her reaction.

"You can't marry him."

"Why not?"

"You just can't."

Peace, holding on to her last vestige of control, slammed out of the room leaving Passion startled and shaken.

One week later Passion and Ben were married.

Exactly sixteen months after they recited their wedding vows, Ben enlisted in the army. Why he enlisted isn't clear. He wasn't particularly patriotic; he thought the war a mistake. Maybe his impulsive gesture was a reaction proportional to the intensity of his love for Passion, a way of proving he was more exciting than the not-very-interesting-middle-aged-man he felt she had married. Or maybe he just wanted an excuse to get away, his years of bachelorhood leaving him unprepared for life with another person, as much as he loved his accommodating wife.

So on June 15, 1965, he left to train at Fort Dix and then, a year later, to join the 200,000 American troops already in Vietnam. Once there he found himself stationed behind the front lines in Danang, where the army, in one of their more intelligent moves, realizing he would serve best in a support position, promoted him to corporeal and placed him in the quartermaster corps. It became Ben's job to make sure the combatants were outfitted with the latest in battle gear. It was not exactly what he had fancied when he first decided to become a hero to his new bride, but after seeing what war was really like, it was a job for which he was grateful.

Naturally, he left out these details when he wrote Passion his lurid narratives of war and pursuit.

After more than a year of marriage, Passion had settled happily into her daily routine with a man who had turned out to be as devoted a husband as promised. Passion hated violence of any kind and war, particularly the Vietnam war, represented to her violence at its worst. As shocked as she was by Ben's decision to enlist in the army, she was even more disappointed in her husband's seemingly endless lust for battle, totally unaware of his actual occupation tending loose buttons and misplaced boots.

So they lied to each other in elaborate detail. Both terrified at being found lacking.

Peace, on the other hand, was delighted. When she learned Ben had enlisted, she could hardly contain herself. The intruder was leaving, perhaps... No, not even she could think such a horrible thought, not even she, but there it was, poking out its ugly head, unstoppable, the intruder was leaving, perhaps...for good. Now she thought to herself, she would have her sister back, and everything could return to normal.

But, of course, it couldn't—and didn't. Things rarely if ever return to normal, and there was a war going on, and it was beginning to be felt even as far away as East Ninth Street, The Lower East Side (now known at The East Village), Manhattan.

Before Ben went off to Vietnam, the war had not affected their lives directly. Before the mid-60's, the Vietnam War had a place in very few people's consciousness or conscience. The Cuban Missile crisis and then Kennedy's assassination on November 22, 1963, were what preoccupied people in those days. Although America was already involved in the conflict, it was an involvement few knew about and even fewer cared about. Soon it would seem there was nothing in the headlines but the war in Vietnam and its effect on everything from the concurrent struggles in the universities to the civil rights movement.

Ben, reading about the events taking place at home from his solitary bunk, worried about Passion. He was sorry now he had enlisted, wanted only to be with her in this difficult time. The war was nothing like he thought it would be, his place in it embarrassing at best. However, still feeling the compulsion to prove his courage to Passion, he continued writing her long letters detailing exploits that would have taxed the imagination of the most diligent Hollywood screenwriter. Scenes of battle, fields of carnage, himself decked out in army regalia armed with full metal jackets, leading the charge of the Twentieth Century light brigade.

Passion in the meantime had joined the peace movement. She was appalled by Ben's letters, couldn't believe the man who had wooed her, who she loved for his gentleness and kindness, had turned into a thoughtless, bloodthirsty killer. She contemplated divorce; she contemplated suicide; she contemplated murder. Nonetheless, she wrote him back letters full of compassion, empathy and love.

She was, after all, his wife.

And she still loved him.

But it was getting harder all the time. Unfortunately, Ben and Passion were on a collision course of contending fantasies.

In such a desperate situation, both at home and in Vietnam, reality was too grim not to intervene. Passion was fast losing her innocence and was slowly beginning to live up to her name. Ben was also losing his, surrounded as he was daily by the very scenes he described so graphically to Passion. He just didn't happen to be involved in them in the heroic way he enunciated with so much vigor. He went on day after day sorting clothes, checking records, watching the occupants of wardrobes he ordered and gave out with such care being brought back clothed simply in a body bag, a job it fell on him to oversee.

As a reward he got promoted. His new nickname became Sergeant Bodybags. Another detail he neglected to include in his letters to Passion.

Their lies were fast overtaking the truth of their lives and were well on the way to destroying their marriage when fate intervened in Ben's favor. A stray bomb from an American bomber over—or, in this case, under—shot its target and came crashing down not far from the complex of buildings that served as Ben's headquarters. Ben was wounded in the thigh by shrapnel and suffered a damaged eardrum, injuries just serious enough to earn him a one-way ticket home.

Passion, learning of his imminent arrival, was first overjoyed and then dismayed. What would happen when her soldier-husband found out the truth? She still loved him, at least the memory of him as he was when he courted and married her. But now? Now was just one big question mark.

The initial meeting of the two lovers after Ben's return was strained and despite kisses and protestations of love, clearly distant. One night, after three weeks of uncomfortable silence, Ben decided to tell Passion the truth. Passion, who had hidden all her peace placards and leaflets and was agonizing over how to tell her wounded husband her own surprising story, couldn't have been more relieved.

After their mutual confessions, they fell into each other's arms.

The war dragged on almost ten more years, during which time New Yorkers changed the color of their clothing and hair styles and changed them back again—men's hair grew long, women's short, then men started cutting their hair and women letting their's grow. Clothing went from black to colorful tie-dye then back again to black. By the late Sixties, poetry readings had been superseded by multimedia happenings, jazz by rock and roll, and peace marches by militant demonstrations.

Ben and Passion decided not to wait to start their family. Their first baby, Arthur, was born exactly nine months and three weeks after Ben returned home—the three weeks being the time it took them to make up.

Peace never married. She had a past filled with too many men to be considered an old maid, and since her sister was the only human being she had ever really enjoyed living with, she decided she would rather live alone and continue to change her male companions seasonally. She had a fall friend, a winter friend, a summer friend and a spring friend—she now took the slogan, "Make Love Not War" seriously. She resolved to fight less and love more, particularly her nieces and nephews who she doted on, constantly making up excuses to bring them a little gifts, until there were so many little Bens and Passions, she could no longer afford off-season presents and stuck to the more traditional holidays.

Altogether Passion and Ben had a total of six children. All, it must be added, with much more conventional names.

THE MAGICIAN & THE POET

Jennifer was an escape artist. Her life was devoted to avoiding traps. She was better than Isaac Bashevis Singer's Magician of Lubin, an ordinary man with an extraordinary way with locks. Unlike him, Jennifer's powers were the result of careful, disciplined study; they were not even vaguely supernatural. And unlike Houdini, her idol, her conundrums were neither mechanical nor physical. It was the highways and byways of the human imagination she scavenged—always in search of a way out. If you asked her what she was trying so hard to get out of, she could not have told you. She only knew that it was important to hone her skills, ply her trade. Sometimes she set traps for herself, just to practice. Traps that became increasingly difficult over time. After all, most of the excitement was generated by the fear that this might be the one time when escape was impossible.

If there was ever anyone who was the exact opposite of Jennifer, it was Alexander. He was a poet. Rather than being an expert at escape, Alexander prided himself on the number of entanglements he could accumulate. There were so many over a period of years he began to think of them in terms of weight rather than number. So many gross pounds of love lost, desire unfulfilled. Alexander was in love with Jennifer. He loved Jennifer as only a true poet can love. If asked, he would have talked about the intricacies and complexities of his feeling for her, not as a puzzle to be solved, or a possession to be treasured, but as the way light moves through forbidden leaves in the twilight hours of a warm Spring night.

Like all true poets, Alexander was an incurable romantic.

Circumstance is nothing if not ironic. Jennifer's downfall came not from her relationship with Alexander, but in the innocent enough looking package of her neighbor, Rachel. Jennifer and Rachel had known each other on and off for years. They were not close friends. They were more like close acquaintances. Jennifer lived in the building that fronted Rachel's. They saw each other occasionally throwing out the garbage, at block parties, tenants meetings. Each encounter was punctuated with a polite nod of the head, a quick hello. Nothing more.

Then one day, or rather one night, Jennifer fell in love. It happened as the result of a seemingly innocuous event. At a meeting called to inform a new tenant of her rights, Rachel's hand brushed Jennifer's as they simultaneously reached for a copy of the rent guidelines, causing the booklet to slide to the floor. In unison, they bent to retrieve it, nearly colliding in the process. Hours later Jennifer could still feel the exact place on her hand that Rachel's hand had touched. This woman, who for years she had never noticed, now became central in her thoughts. Almost immediately, dread accompanied by a rush of excitement, Jennifer recognized the ultimate trap, the one from which there might be no escape.

It was not that Jennifer had never thought about making love to a woman before. After all, to limit experience was to limit the thrill of discovery. Mostly, though, her affections had been aimed squarely in the direction of the male of the species, a position she was most comfortable with, despite her complaints, and one where, most important, she felt in control.

Jennifer's relationship with Alexander was much more direct. They had gone out to dinner a few times, to a movie, and then to bed. The differences between Alexander and Jennifer, although pronounced, were more a matter of temperament and interest than gender. Or maybe it was really a matter of timing, Alexander moving to a slower, more leisurely beat, wanting to hold and prolong each moment, to stretch it beyond its limits—and most people's patience.

Alexander and Jennifer had one thing in common. They both thought frequently—although neither would have admitted it—about sex. While Alexander constructed dream edifices of dialogue, Jennifer's focus was much more mundane. As she became more interested in Rachel, her attention slowly shifted from male to female anatomy. Her daydreams became populated with soft breasts and gently curving thighs.

Jennifer didn't like to think of the objects of her affections as prey, but it was hard to get away from the hunting metaphor. Once captured, everything rested on the ability of the individual in question to slip past her. Her victims were her teachers. It was from them she learned the techniques of evasion.

Alexander, on the other hand, had no sense of the temporal, therefore he lacked the ability to excel in linear pursuits. The idea of getting from A to B to C was foreign to his nature. His psyche was like a huge amoebae that nourished itself by drawing everything in and absorbing it. Every day as Jennifer grew leaner, he grew more ample. As she withdrew more from the world, it became a larger part of him.

Because Rachel was also attracted to Jennifer, she slowly began to make herself available to her. She would just happen to be throwing out the garbage at the exact time Jennifer was coming home. She made sure to sit next to Jennifer at the weekly tenants' meeting and finally, at one of the meetings, suggested that Jennifer might like to come over to her apartment to see the blueprints that had been drawn up for the neighborhood garden they were planning for the vacant lot on the corner of Ninth Street and Avenue C.

Two nights later Rachel and Jennifer made love.

It was finally with Rachel that Jennifer found a lover whose touch resonated with familiarity, whose kisses sank into, rather than glided off of the surfaces of her skin. Instead of her imagination, Jennifer could now rely on memory to embellish her dreams.

Rachel and Alexander should have been enemies. Instead they became friends. They shared a common experience and neither crossed the other's boundaries. That isn't to say they spent much time together or confided in each other, simply that they were cordial to each other and meant it. Maybe they sensed even then what the future held and that jealousy in their particular case didn't make much sense.

As time went on, Jennifer began to realize just how much she had come to depend on Rachel, to need her. Their relationship was no longer a tactical problem that promised a complex but rewarding solution. The tension this produced became intolerable. Jennifer ceased having fantasies of pursuit and desire. Her mind turned instead to far-off places, a new city perhaps, a different job. She began to call Alexander in the middle of the night, detailing elaborate plans for adventures the two of them could undertake. Alexander at first was delighted. It seemed all his fantasies were finally coming true. But soon he too began to get frightened. This was too real.

People who live in close proximity often exchange pieces of their personality, much in the same way they borrow each other's clothes, until finally they can be seen walking the streets unconsciously wearing their newly acquired attitudes like a sleeve that appears strangely faded, a shoe that doesn't quite fit. It produces a noticeable awkwardness that is evident to those astute enough to see it. With Jennifer and Alexander, it was an equal exchange. As Jennifer became more passive, Alexander became more confident. He began to see his situation as something of a challenge, not at all the romantic adventure he had at first believed, but nothing to be afraid of either. He became less poetic and more practical. He finally proposed to Jennifer that they move in together, find a bigger apartment, leave Ninth Street altogether.

Rachel immediately noticed the change in Jennifer. She could feel her drawing away from her. Rachel woke up one night startled to find the face lying beside her that of a stranger. The sensation passed quickly, but left her with a great sadness, a sense of overwhelming loss.

Jennifer finally agreed to leave with Alexander. After all, a poet and a magician belong together, even if he had stopped writing poetry and she no longer cared about snares and traps. Jennifer knew he was her last chance at escape. Life with Alexander might be dull, but she would never lose herself in him. Her victory might be a sham, but it was a victory all the same.

Rachel, in the meantime, wondered if she would ever again hear the sound of her beloved sea. Everything around her was suddenly silent. When she spoke, she could not hear her own voice. People around her moved their lips, but the noise that came from their mouths held no meaning for her. Rachel knew in time the world that was so dear to her would return. But it would be different. Everything had changed.

THE PARTY

Margaret Hansen constructed her world meticulously, as an extension of herself. In this her imagination was essential. And what an imagination it was! Not of the extraordinary, the fantastic. No, Margaret's imagination was a compendium of the minute details of daily existence, details that taken one by one would be boring, but juxtaposed in a way that only an artist can, ignoring logic, form, her imagination overflowed until the world around her took on her shape.

Every day presented Margaret with a new dilemma to be solved. She moved from place to place the way one moves the pieces of a jigsaw puzzle, gathering pieces with corresponding colors, looking for the appropriate shape, trying and retrying to fit each piece, the borders first and then building slowly, working from the edges to the center.

In other words, what for someone else might seem easy was for her a trying, but challenging exercise.

Her favorite activity was giving parties. She imagined herself the Mrs. Dalloway of Ninth Street. Of course, she didn't have Mrs. Dalloway's money or position, fictitious as they were, but she imagined she had her flair for inviting the appropriate guests, joining each one as she joined the pieces of the giant puzzle she kept in what passed for her living room. She kept all the names, addresses and phone numbers of each of the tenants in the building on 3x5 cards filed in a black and white speckled oblong box— along with every person she had ever met and admired enough to ask for personal information. Each day she would rifle through the names imagining all sorts of combinations of faces, voices, interests. So when it was announced that the building on Ninth Street was scheduled for demolition, she felt it was her duty, her sacred trust, in fact, to provide the farewell party.

The very next morning after notices had been posted on each tenant's door, she took out the small group of names she had collected under the title *Tenants* and carefully laid them out on the table, arranging them in different patterns as one might arrange a deck of Tarot cards, as if the arrangement itself had the power to unlock the mysteries of the past, present and future of each of the participants.

Since it was a farewell party, she felt she should invite everyone in the two buildings—the large front building, the small back structure. Or should she? After all, this party had to be perfect, or as close to perfection as possible. Who knew what the future held for her, how many more parties, if any, she might give. But if she did leave someone out, who should it be?

Perhaps Mr. Jones, the tenant who lived in 1A. He kept pretty much to himself, no one really knew him. She wasn't even sure how he would act at a party. Maybe he was a closet drunk, or even worse, a drug addict who would go berserk.

It wasn't likely. In reality, he was a small, quiet man who only appeared three or four times a day to walk a dog as small and quiet as he was. He was old enough to be retired, living off Social Security or a pension plan. She knew very little about him even though she had lived there almost fifty years, and he almost thirty.

No, there was no real reason to exclude Mr. Jones, even with his pathetic name. Margaret didn't believe anyone was really named Jones, or Smith for that matter. It was obviously an alias. Still there *was* no real reason to exclude him, and he might turn out to be interesting after all. Maybe surrounded by the conviviality of neighbors he had carefully managed to avoid all these years, he would break down and tell interesting tales of an early life, adventures no one expected a "Jones" could ever have.

Margaret put her pencil down on the table, angling it carefully parallel to the stack of cards. She loved order. Aesthetics for her was order. Another reason her parties had to be just right.

As she reached for her pencil, she froze for a moment, bewildered. Slowly turning her head from side to side, as if seeing the familiar objects in her room for the first time, she tried to locate herself in a room that had suddenly become strange. She felt heavy. A feeling she often had now. It was amazing how one day you could walk up a flight of stairs and think nothing of it, and the next it would be a gigantic task just to lift your foot up one stair and then another, the top of the flight seemingly endless, and when you finally arrived you couldn't help a tiny groan—hoping no one would hear—escaping from your lips.

She remembered—how few years ago it seemed now—when she could dance, light on her feet, as if suspended above gravity, as if the earth had no pull on her at all. Even now it was not the earth that pulled her, it was the weight of her own body that pushed against it.

Margaret was not overweight, she was actually too thin for her five foot frame. But heavy was still the right word. She felt the heaviness you feel when your eyes are heavy, when sleep is urgent.

Margaret shook herself, as if to shake herself out of the lethargy that threatened to overcome her. Maybe she had been concentrating too hard on her plans. But usually when she was as excited as she felt now, energy was no problem.

She remembered how she had made fun of Sadie the afternoon Sadie had taken a cab home—that day seemed years ago now—when she only worked a few blocks away, complaining how her legs suddenly felt like weights, how hard it was to move them. Margaret had gossiped to her neighbors, to Helen who worked in the grocery store down the street, that it had all finally caught up with Sadie, the pounds of lox and cream cheese and halvah and all the other goodies she sold, that Sadie was getting old, getting fat, getting lazy.

Margaret remembered how Rachel had caught her one day imitating Sadie, the incongruity of her imitation, waddling like a duck but with the imperious air of royalty. How furious Rachel had been. The "Imperial Duck" she had called her, a nickname that Margaret could swear she heard her neighbors whispering as she passed by. And now here she was, weighted down herself, heavy, heavy...

So heavy…

The street was almost empty, punctuated with bright bits of newspapers and beer cans, remnants of late night dinners festering in the summer heat—a city feast for pigeons, sparrows and rodents, both squirrels and rats. She knew it was Sunday because precisely at 11:00 the stillness was broken by the sound of a single church bell summoning parishioners to morning prayer at Middle Collegiate Church, its mellow solitary tones tedious, but strangely comforting, in stark contrast to remembered sharp quick echoes of crowd-filled Saturday nights.

Margaret had often wondered how her memories would correspond to reality if she could somehow travel back in time. She felt little had altered over the last fifty years, but maybe that was because she had walked these streets every day, living them from minor change to minor change.

And now, miraculously, here she was, standing at the corner of Seventh Street and Second Avenue, fifty years in the past. And yes, it did look surprisingly the same. Seventh, one of the quieter streets in the neighborhood, had barely changed, at least in outward appearance.

Despite the glare of the mid-morning sun, color seemed strangely muted, the first indication of difference. Turning to face the avenue, she saw no young people wandering down Second Avenue sporting purple spiked hair, tattoos or endless chain adornments on their way home or to a late breakfast or the laundromat. The extravagantly colorful dress of the late '60s and '70s was in the future. With the exception of the fedoras sported by the older men, the fact that none of the women were wearing trousers, and the absence of sneakers, even the way people dressed was almost indistinguishable from her own time. The automobiles parked on the streets looked old to her and very large even though some of them were obviously brand new, and the lack of parking meters was noticeable.

Funny, how something as seemingly mundane as the presence or lack of parking meters could take on such significance.

Otherwise, it all did look much as she had imagined. But that's where the familiarity ended. As she turned and walked east toward Avenue B and her apartment on Ninth Street, she realized how alien the landscape felt that confronted her. The fact that it looked so familiar added to her anxiety. It was as if she had been thrown into a setting that duplicated everything she was used to but was, in essence, totally foreign.

She began to panic. She was suddenly afraid any moment ev-erything around her would shatter, would leave her standing frozen in the midst of broken bits of trees and houses and people cascading around her like the packs of playing cards at the conclusion of Alice in Wonderland.

But Alice had been in a strange and monstrous place. For Marga-ret, this Wonderland she found herself in was all the more frightening because she recognized every landmark, every store, even remembered buildings that would be seen there in the future. What should have been comforting was distressing, like returning home after a long ab-sence eager for the warmth and ease of a place totally your own, to find what should have been the most welcoming was the strangest and most frightening and needed living in all over again to once more make it yours.

Margaret knew instinctively as she left the relative safety of Sev-enth Street the differences would become even more apparent. A shop front might have been altered, restaurant after restaurant might have replaced stationery stores, cleaners, newsstands—the original occupants of the neighborhood—but the street itself, the buildings themselves, for the most part, had not changed. And that would make the dissociation she was experiencing even more vivid.

She looked around anxiously, as if she could feel the presence of all the people who would populate this particular space in the next fifty years pressing in around her. She felt her heart begin to pound, a cold sweat mist her face.

She looked into the window of Anthony's Shoe Repair, saw her reflection superimposed over the rows of weathered shoes waiting to be polished, resoled, restored to near-original luster, curious to see if she too had been transformed magically into herself as she was fifty years before. But no, reflected back at her was the same tired face that had confronted her that morning.

And then the most frightening thought of all occurred to her. What if she should see herself walking toward her? That young girl with all her hope and expectations. What would she do? Even worse, what if she did not recognize herself? What if that alienation, that lack of connection, that disassociation extended even to her own past self?

She could not imagine anything more horrifying.

Margaret was sorry now she had ever returned, had ever wished to return. Actuality replacing nostalgia, the past held no comfort for her. She wanted to go back to where she came from—or more accurately forward.

But she couldn't.

Stuck in memory, she could only pray with time it would all become familiar to her once again...

It was a week before the super, sent over by the landlord to collect Margaret's late rent, found her. Ringing her bell in vain, he took it upon himself to break into her apartment, feeling something must indeed be wrong with an old lady who, in the fifty odd years she had lived in Apartment 16 had never, no, not even once, been late with her rent. A woman who was so punctual in all she did that her neighbors joked they could set their watches by her comings and goings.

Searching through each room in turn, he finally found Margaret slumped over her kitchen table, four piles of cards neatly stacked in rows pillowing her chin, her eyes open, staring at the freshly papered wall, her head supported by the dozens of names she had kept so diligently for years.

THE END OF AN ERA

Rachel's downstairs neighbor Sadie was the only tenant to have lived at 630 E. 9th Street longer than Rachel. She had successfully run a delicatessen on Second Avenue between Fifth and Sixth Streets until her husband Mo died of a heart attack one night after putting away his third roast beef and coleslaw sandwich on rye.

Sadie had managed to keep the store open for a year after Mo's untimely death, but had finally given up. Not because the work was too hard, but because without her husband it was no longer any fun. Making sandwich after endless sandwich, smiling at customers she no longer cared to see, lost all attraction for her. She felt she was drowning in numbers—the cost of herring and coleslaw, the pounds of smoked fish and large, dense loaves of bread. It all seemed to sink into her feet, until one day she had to call for help to get to the door, locking it forever before she hailed a cab to go the few short blocks she had always before walked home.

Unlike Rachel, Sadie hated detail. Unlike Rachel, Sadie was content with her life. She felt after so many years of pickles and cream cheese, customers and husbands, she deserved a rest, even if it turned out to be her last. She loved being home doing nothing. She lived now without clocks.

Sadie and Rachel were great friends.

Often at night, the two of them would sit in Rachel's kitchen drinking endless cups of herbal tea. Sadie would pet Rachel's cat, her feet resting comfortably on an unused chair. She would tell Rachel stories about the customers who had passed through the glass doors of her store demanding bagels and conversation, coffee and a friendly smile. Sadie had become for them, even more than the wares in her store, a welcome routine, a map they could reckon their week by, something calming in a ruthless workaday world.

Sadie had lived in the neighborhood her entire life. The truth is at this point she wouldn't know how to live anywhere else. Maybe that's why she got along so well with Rachel's cat, Jezebel. They both understood territory.

Like many New Yorkers, Sadie could exist happily within the radius of a few square blocks, rarely venturing further except occasionally to shop, go to a movie, or indulge in one of her favorite pastimes, a ride on the Staten Island Ferry—a treat her husband Mo had introduced her to when they were courting.

The East Village. How she and Rachel laughed over that realtors' term, coined to sell apartments to a clientele wary of the immigrant, working-class connotations of a neighborhood called "The Lower East Side." Words that had no negative connotation for Sadie, straddling as she did two generations—her parents' and that of the "new immigrants," the young artists and students, poets and playwrights and actors and activists she lived among now.

She and Mo had never had children, but if they had they would have been about the age of these serious young people who frequented her bialys and bagels, bringing with them the talent and enthusiasm that had inspired her in her own youth during the heyday of the Yiddish theater: the excitement of evenings spent at the Molly Picone Theater on Twelfth Street or the Anderson Theater a few blocks away; seeing Shakespeare and Chekhov for the first time—albeit adaptations tempered with a few added songs and an obligatory happy ending.

Sadie, even at sixty, was too young to remember legendary performances of "The Yeshiva Student," a musical adaptation of Shakespeare's "Hamlet," but she was just old enough to have seen her favorite, "The Dybbuk." She felt a deep affinity with Chanon, the Dybbuk's tragic hero, caught as he was between two worlds. She would cry, remembering the romance of it all, the yearning that followed the lovers even into death.

Those were the days when Second Avenue was "uptown," a place you went to party and forget for a time the grayness of Orchard Street or Eldridge Street or Rivington or Essex, the rank odor that threatened even the most obstinate humor, pervading streets swarming with vendors, children, garment workers. Decades later, when cars had replaced pushcarts and a medley of new languages had replaced the Yiddish and Ladino and occasional Italian that permeated the streets, she could still smell that unmistakable stench.

For Sadie, her delicatessen was a family legacy. Her parents had owned a small bakery on Delancy Street adjacent to the Williamsburg Bridge. At the entrance to the bridge was a small pedestrian area where, weather permitting, she ate lunch, often accompanied by Mo who romanced her over challah and knishes until she finally agreed to marry him. When they got an opportunity to rent a space for their own store on Second Avenue, they pooled their money and left her crowded family apartment on Rivington and Essex to set up housekeeping on Ninth Street, close enough that she could walk the short distance to Second Avenue.

The first thing Sadie did when they moved to Ninth Street was paint her new apartment the brightest white she could find. There were two colors she detested: green and maroon. The dark, drab colors of her childhood. She had forbidden Mo to hang the rose embellished wallpaper he had bought for their new bedroom, reminding her as it did of the crowded floral walls that imprisoned her as she was growing up.

More than anything else, Sadie craved light. Her family's small three room apartment had been filled with oversized mahogany furniture, always padded with maroon or green velveteen cushions, the same color as the living room and kitchen walls. Mahogany represented to them the comfortable upper middle class American life they dreamed of and saved for. Mahogany was the color of wealth.

Mo never understood why she was so vehement. Mo. How she missed him! When they were together she often forgot he was there, although he might be only a foot away from her, carving the long, shining cuts of lox into paper-thin transparent slices. It was odd, in his absence she felt him as a tangible presence more than she had when he was standing so comfortably beside her.

Sadie's life might have seemed to some commonplace, dull, living vicariously as she did through the gossip and small talk of her patrons, as she literally sliced their daily bread. But Sadie always scoffed at people who suggested she was the personification of a first-generation Lower East Side resident.

She understandably resented being considered a cliché.

Only from the outside, she would say. Only from the outside. You could wander into a neighbor's home by mistake and for a moment think it was yours. The same furniture, the same wallpaper, the same color paint on the walls. But we were different inside, she would say. All of us. Nothing alike. We lived inside, not like now, everything on the outside different, everything on the inside the same.

For many, Sadie's retirement and eventual demise signified the end of an era, the collapse of a generation. Rachel missed her dearly. Sadie's friendship was a quiet place where Rachel could gather her thoughts, store her past. Sadie had become, in many ways, her home.

RACHEL SAYS GOODBYE

Jezebel was Rachel's faithful cat. Well, as faithful as any cat can be expected to be—which is more faithful than most people think. Jezebel, as the wise old cat she was, knew many truths, and by the same token many fallacies, including the one about animals and unconditional love.

That an animal's love is unconditional is a delusion, Jezebel thought, as she absentmindedly cleaned her paw. Abuse a cat, or a dog, and they will eventually turn on you or hide from you. What cats in particular do sublimely well is allow humans to love them unconditionally. And, as the fastidious cat she was, Jezebel was very careful about who she allowed to love her. It was a privilege she granted only to Rachel.

Rachel did love Jezebel, and Jezebel considered Rachel part of her family, although she was a little confused just where Rachel fit in. Sometimes she thought of Rachel as an errant kitten; sometimes Jezebel mixed Rachel up with her mother because Rachel groomed and fed her the way her mother had when she was a kitten. Jezebel particularly liked the short wire brush Rachel used to make her coat shiny and rid her of all the itchy hairs that constantly tormented her. Jezebel knew this whole thing humans had about cats' independence was another popular myth. Cats aren't independent, they are just impossible or nearly impossible to train.

At this thought, if cats could laugh, Jezebel would have laughed.

But cats are experts *at* training. And since she had trained Rachel so easily—where to scratch her neck, when and where and what to feed her—she suspected Rachel couldn't be a cat. Jezebel wasn't quite sure what the alternative was, but then she didn't think about it too much. Cats are not known for being philosophical.

Jezebel loved to hunt. Rachel had decided for safety's sake to keep her indoors where there was more than enough to do to keep her occupied. Before Jezebel had arrived the apartment had been overrun by mice. Once Jezebel had been loaned to a downstairs neighbor to kill a rat. A huge rat. What a battle that had been. Jezebel purred and licked her fur vigorously thinking about it. That was a battle worth relating. Sometimes when Rachel was brushing her and Jezebel felt in a particularly good mood she would purr her deeds of prowess and cunning to remind Rachel what an exemplary companion she had.

That's how Jezebel felt about Rachel, but how did Rachel feel about Jezebel?

Rachel often looked at Jezebel lying contentedly in the exact spot where she was about to sit, or on a pile of papers she was sorting, or on the bed watching TV, and thought how often the cat had saved her sanity. There was something comforting about living with a domesticated animal who exhibited so many features of the wild—an observation which would have caused Jezebel, who hardly thought of herself as domesticated, to chuckle again. Rachel marveled at how the two of them, creatures from completely different species, could communicate, when it was so hard for her to communicate with her own kind. Perhaps it was because Jezebel's needs were so simple. To be loved, fed, and when she desired it, left alone.

Rachel was more like Jezebel than she knew. Underneath her longing for a home, for someone to share her life with besides her faithful cat, was an independence that gnawed and tugged at her relentlessly. She had been married once briefly, had moved to the Upper West Side with her new husband full of dreams of a future of security and children, but had felt lost among the tall apartment buildings, their cramped metal elevators and artificial greenery. She had instigated a quarrel just to have an excuse to escape to her old neighborhood. Rachel returned contrite after a few days, but knew the relationship was doomed.

One night when it was raining so hard it was impossible to sleep, the rain pounding relentlessly on the roof—one of the only disadvantages of her top floor apartment—she found Jezebel, or Jezebel found her. Hearing a persistent loud meowing on the fire escape that doubled as her front stairs, Rachel made the "mistake"—a name she often called Jezebel when angry at her—of putting out a dish of tuna she had left over from lunch. From then on every few nights Jezebel would return for an evening meal. Bumblebee albacore was replaced by Figaro chunk, but Jezebel didn't seem to care, fish was fish. It beat the garbage and scraps she was used to.

The unusual thing about Jezebel was that she was actually quite an elegant cat. A large calico with gleaming white fur, she had an exceptionally smooth and glistening coat. Rachel was sure some anxious owner was looking for her, so she tacked up signs around the neighborhood; but nobody responded, and Rachel never saw any notices for a missing cat of Jezebel's type. Since Jezebel had already decided she would allow Rachel to care for her, with a contented meow she settled in to become an indispensable part of Rachel's household. Which came as a surprise to Rachel if not to Jezebel, who took it for granted in the manner of her kind.

Jezebel lived with Rachel, or rather allowed Rachel to live with her, for almost ten years. But like many humans, Jezebel got the cat equivalent of the seven-year—in this case ten-year—itch. One day, gazing fondly at the great outdoors through half closed eyes, or more accurately, gazing fondly at the adjacent vacant lot littered with garbage, and unable to block out the insistent cry of her sisters and brothers perched on the back alley fence, craving the "call of the wild" and a good old-fashioned cat fight— how she purred thinking about that, back hairs bristling, ears laid back, oh heaven—even knowing that leaving Rachel might mean a quick end to her now comfortable life, Jezebel squeezed gracefully through an open window and vigorously shaking herself sallied forth proudly to take her chances once again in the wide world.

Maybe she thought in the back of her small cat brain that one day when she tired again, she would either find another Rachel or return, a prodigal daughter, to be welcomed with open arms and Figaro tuna—not knowing that soon there would be no 630 East Ninth Street to return to.

So on a sunny day in November, the leaves slowly beginning to turn as they prepared to litter the cement with their splendor, Rachel came home to find Jezebel gone. She searched the neighborhood frantically for days, stapling and taping flyers, stopping everyone on the street, sitting in the park for hours, hoping, hoping, but it was no use. The cat had vanished as mysteriously as she had arrived.

For Rachel, whose relationship with Jezebel had been the longest she had ever known, it was a devastating blow. Friends, fearing for her health, suggested she get another cat, perhaps a kitten this time, one who would bond with her and not have the wanderlust of a street cat, no matter how aristocratic and beautiful. Jezebel, after all, had grown up in the alleys and comfortable as Rachel's home was, as much as she loved Rachel, she would always remain bound to danger and garbage.

This was no criticism of Jezebel, so aptly named, it was simply a fact.

Like many of the people in my life, Rachel thought. Somehow weaving their own stories in which I might temporarily play a character, but no more than that. A character in someone else's story. Even my cat's.

No use thinking along those lines. After all, she was living a story too, and at least she could play the main character in that tale. So one day, after a month and two weeks, Rachel took down the few flyers that were still left tacked up in stores, and praying that Jezebel would either find happiness in her new found freedom or find another home where she would be appreciated for the magnificent animal she was, and not end up a cat statistic, Rachel started to sort through her few belongings in preparation for her own journey in search of a new, if not better, home.

The Sea. How beautiful it seemed to Rachel. Ocean edged by shore, the way the sand waits, patient, then turns and glides inward guided by waves. The way she would have liked to wait. For what? For anything at all. Even the years that advanced toward her

Is that what forgetfulness is? she thought to herself as she packed, looking around her room for one last time. The advancing and retreating of years, the ebbing of time? The respite we all long for, and distrust?

The morning the pigeon nested under her air-conditioner was the morning she finally decided to move. It was a foregone conclusion anyway. They were tearing down the building to make way for a new high-rise and there wasn't anything that Rachel or the tenants' association could do about it. She knew that now. Her cousin in Albuquerque had been writing her for years about the virtues of the desert.

Anyway, you aren't getting any younger, you know.

Rachel hated leaving her old apartment and the ocean that sang to her so conveniently, that might or might not follow her to a more western region. The desert and the ocean, were they compatible? Well, unless she tried, she would never find out.

And so, one morning, she finished packing the one small bag she had decided to take with her and locked her door a final time. If Nirvana were to be found, it could be found anywhere. Any place, or no place, like the ocean she loved so well.

AN AFTERWORD
9TH STREET
THE SPIRIT OF A NEIGHBORHOOD

Rona L. Holub

Nirvana on Ninth Street reflects a time and a place that existed for a little over two decades in the second half of the twentieth-century. As Susan Sherman suggests through the voice of East 9th Street, that time was but a brief moment in the street's long history. Today, East 9th Street is positioned in the area of Manhattan dubbed the East Village that borders Houston Street to the south, Fourteenth Street to the north, Third Avenue to the west, and the East River to the east. East 9th Street runs through the East Village from Avenue D on the east (blocked from the East River by the Jacob Riis Houses) and on the west to Fifth Avenue (where it becomes West 9th Street, as determined by the 1811 street grid plan).

For nearly a hundred and fifty years, East 9th Street had been situated on the Lower East Side of New York. Like all of the Lower East Side, a large and diverse population arriving during great waves of immigration of the nineteenth and early twentieth centuries lived, worked, played on the streets of this part of the city. Of course, as Sherman's 9th Street lets us know, the first immigrants arrived much earlier; in fact, they landed in the 1600s and this area of Manahattan—named, visited and inhabited by First Peoples, typically of the Lenape nations—became farms owned by Dutch governors, most notably, Peter Stuyvesant. What remains of those immigrants is a plaque on the northwest corner of 13th Street and Third Avenue in honor of a pear tree that once stood on Stuyvesant's land, and a few Dutch place names like the Bowery (*bouwerij*), the anglicized Dutch word for farm. During the largest stream of immigration, the Lower East Side stretched from 14th Street to the north, bordered by the East River to the east and the Bowery to the west, ending in the south at Canal Street.

While East 9th Street remained steadfastly where it had always been, in the 1960s and '70s the street became part of a new area carved out of what was once the sprawling immigrant Lower East Side. It was officially christened the East Village when Rose Ryan, the head of classified advertising at *The Village Voice,* helped re-name the area to encourage ad placements by Lower East Side landlords and area realtors. Real estate interests reasoned that East 9th Street's traditional location in the northern part of the Lower East Side made it unappealing to new renters and developers. The Lower East Side, after all, represented the older, less hip immigrants of yesteryear, not attractive to the more prosperous potential new renters who began arriving after World War II. Thus, an imagined relocation occurred. East 9th Street moved (without, of course, actually moving) from its true Lower East Side home into the new and more exciting "East Village."

Traditionally East 9th Street had been home to working class families, as well as to those struggling for a rung on the ladder, or simply for survival. With its new name, real estate interests hoped that minds could be molded to believe the teeming Lower East Side was actually somehow a "wing" of the much more lilting and quaint-sounding Greenwich Village. Perhaps the East Village would be seen as simply an easterly extension of an area touted as cleaner, more elegant (or at least "cool" or "hip"), a place where writers and artists congregated and beautiful rows of town houses lined the streets. Maybe, the name would conjure up for new inhabitants an entirely different place from the one their grandparents or parents knew; relatives who might themselves have arrived on the Lower East Side fleeing poverty and persecution.

Great energy and a sense of transformation filled Sherman's East 9th Street, informing the cultural renaissance of the 1960s. A large number of immigrants from Poland and the Ukraine still lived alongside African-Americans and newcomers from Puerto Rico and the Dominican Republic, most of whom lived nearer the easternmost border of the East Village. Maurice Schwartz's once famous Yiddish Art Theater still stood unchanged with only the occasional show running. Ukrainian and Polish restaurants—famous for their *pierogis* (boiled or baked stuffed dumplings) that could fill you up at a very low price—still lined the busy streets as *bodegas* popped up alongside them.

A few Italian bakeries remained and the 2nd Avenue Deli offered kosher delicatessen to remaining Jewish Lower East Siders. Ratner's, also on 2nd Avenue, an old fashioned Jewish Dairy Restaurant that observed the Jewish law of not mixing dairy and meat dishes, served the hungry yearning for kosher vegetarian chopped liver. Some people even traveled from the boroughs and tri-state area to eat food resonant with memories. It was much easier then to get a good bowl of borscht, a nice dairy meal, a kosher hot dog and even rice and beans, than it is today.

In the '60s and '70s, the newly minted East Village became home to a different set of immigrants, young people from the boroughs and across the country returning to the freedom of city life, among them artists, writers, dancers, filmmakers, playwrights and musicians. A slow trickle that had begun in the '50s accelerated in the '60s creating a vibrant artistic community. One of the most notable of these early migrants, Allen Ginsberg, lived on East 2nd, 5th, 10th, 12th, and 14th Streets between 1952 and his death in 1997. This New Jersey born and bred author became attached to the area as would so many others.

Some might think of these new arrivals as cultural pioneers bringing art, music and rebellion into the area. In reality, they were only the next wave of wanderers to inhabit this northern part of the Lower East Side. Artists, writers and agitators have always lived on or near East 9th Street, like the author and revolutionary anarchist Emma Goldman, who resided at 208 East 13th Street in the early 20th century before she was forcibly deported as a result of the anti-Communist Palmer Raids of 1919. Thomas Wolfe, Frank O'Hara and e e cummings, as well as musicians Charlie

Parker and the folk legend Leadbelly, had earlier lived in the area.

In the late 1960s and into the '80s, New York City fell into decline. Residents of the East Village, which by the early '70s was decayed and riddled with the problems of neglect and the growing drug trade, lived day to day with the same problems that affected the rest of the city during that period. Runaways escaped to dangerous streets. Drug addicts and dealers used crumbling tenements for business and "pleasure."

During this chaotic era, a different set of immigrants lured by the cheap rents began filling up the vacancies left by the children of older tenants who had fled the city for what they saw as a cleaner, safer suburban way of life. Empty, abandoned buildings filled the East Village, along with the rest of the Lower East Side. Tenants no longer able to pay rent, owners who could not "profitably" rent their buildings, some landlords unable to pay taxes or maintain upkeep, and others finding they could make more money "warehousing" their properties simply left them vacant. Such spaces became home to young, adventurous squatters with little money. Writers, artists, dancers as well as the homeless took to occupying these unwanted "free" spaces.

There is no denying that the city was in trouble in the late '60s and '70s, but it was still a city full of people, enthusiasm, and excitement. Life, as it does, went on. Families worked for a living, children played, people used the streets to meet, talk, organize. With all its problems, the East Village was still a place filled with creativity, intellectual discourse, and political action. It was especially in the 1960s that the East Village attained its own identity, separate from the rest of the Lower East Side. This time, in particular, set the tone for the image of the East Village that remains in the popular imagination.

The East Village also began to become known as a hotbed of increased radicalism and East 9th Street was in the epicenter of the action. Even though it is true that as far back as the nineteenth-century, radical action and rioting took place, often right in Tompkins Square Park during the economic downturns of 1857 and

1873/4 (just two of many recessions, depressions, and panics in a boom and bust century). The police "rioted" in 1874, clubbing and riding through a crowd of peacefully assembled workers, which would not be the last time such excesses on the part of authority would occur. On August 7, 1988, Tompkins Square Park became effectively a war zone when an anti-gentrification demonstration called to protest a midnight curfew in the park erupted into violence when over 450 riot police charged demonstrators, bystanders, residents, tourists, and the homeless, beginning a rampage that lasted until the early hours of the morning and spilled into the adjoining neighborhood, resulting in what amounted to a police occupation of the neighborhood for almost a month. And in 1995, Giuliani sent in a "tank-like armored vehicle" (*NY Times*, 1995) and hundreds of officers to seize two East Village tenements and remove 31 squatters.

Immigrants and migrants to the neighborhood in the '60s established many new institutions, some of which still exist. The well-known Nuyorican Poets Café began in 1973 in an apartment and still provides artistic expression to the community and beyond in their present space on East 3rd Street between Avenues B and C. Poets Miguel Algarín, Miguel Piñero, and Sandra María Estevez were among the founding artists, with roots in the area that became more popularly known among residents as "Losaida." In fact, poet/founder of the Nuyorican Poet's Café, Bimbo Rivas, originated this name for the most easterly part of the area in his 1974 poem of the same name, a place heavily populated by Latinos, predominantly Puerto Rican, who brought and cultivated new cultural riches into the city.

As tough and poor as the entire East Village had become, especially the areas around the lettered avenues, immigrants still settled into its tenements and streets. In an area that had become synonymous with ethnic diversity, action and art, they continued to protest against the Vietnam War, used spaces that had been neglected without official permission, fixed up and planted neglected open lots, and took over buildings, creating homes and community, while creating art and culture.

The creators of the earliest cultural institutions inspired the creation of new institutions throughout the '60s, '70s, and '80s, that exist into the present. To mention just a few, there was The Tenth Street Coffeehouse which morphed into the Deux Megots and later The Metro, meeting places for poets and playwrights in the early and middle '60s, precursors of The St. Mark's Poetry Project which began in 1966 in St. Mark's Church on 10th Street. The Theater for the New City, founded in 1971, is still going strong on First Avenue between 9th and 10th Streets, as is La Mama ETC founded by Ellen Stewart now located on E. 4th Street between 3rd and 4th Avenues, next to where IKONbooks once flourished as a cultural hub and movement center in the late '60s and early '70s. CBGBs on the Bowery near Bleecker is now defunct but bolstered and supported the careers of the Ramones, Patti Smith, Joan Jett and others of the Punk and New Wave Scene; and PS 122 opened its doors in 1979 and has just received an overhaul.

The Gathering of the Tribes, a space for artistic and cultural exploration, originating in 1991 as part of poet Steve Cannon's apartment, continues on East 3rd. The Bowery Poetry Club was founded in 2002 by Bob Holman, who at one time was a co-director of the Nuyorican Poets Café, and The Museum of Reclaimed Urban Space at 155 Aveue C, right in the heart of Losaida, recently began offering tours and exhibits that educate about grassroots activism of squatters and local residents revitalizing vacant lots and buildings for the community.

And, not to be overlooked, right on the corner of East 9th Street and Second Avenue in the East Village is Veselka, where that rare bowl of borscht (cold available during the summer months) can still be enjoyed. The restaurant itself is run by descendants of Ukrainian immigrants who opened it in 1954. It is an updated and expanded version of its former self, a business that survived the years of struggle, always vibrant with conversation and energy, whether in 1963 or 2014, surviving the good, bad and ugly of the ups and downs, declines and transformations of East Village/9th Street history.

The E 9th Street in *Nirvana* was located between Avenues B and C in the area real estate brokers would once again rename, this time to "Alphabet City." As the name implies, it is an area made up of the only lettered avenues in the entire city. They thought once again a new name might appeal to prospective tenants of the expensive condos in newly "appropriated" buildings around Tompkins Square Park and further the gentrification process which escalated during the more "prosperous" 90s.

And what of the East Village/Alphabet City/Losaida in 2014? More and more houses and even blocks are being demolished to build large apartment complexes and dorms, exorbitant rents are being charged as tenants of rent-controlled apartments leave or die and rent stabilization is eroded more at every rent stabilization board meeting. Giant glass structures invade Third Avenue and threaten to encroach ever eastward replacing four and five story dwellings crowding out the remnants of the diverse population that once resided in them. Much of the artistic fervor of the neighborhood has moved to the borders and finally out of the neighborhood altogether. But cultural gathering places like La Mama, Tribes, the Bowery Poetry Club, Dixon Place and the Nuyorican are still alive and flourishing. What the future of the neighborhood holds only time will tell.

The fictional and sometimes fantastic stories in *Nirvana on Ninth Street* mirror the emotions, decisions, interactions, of the people who once lived on these streets. Quite clearly it takes a poet to capture the essence of an area that is much more complex and complicated than a surface read can capture, and in this collection, Susan Sherman has done just that.

ACKNOWLEDGMENTS

I would like like to thank Deborah Pintonelli for constructive comments that helped shape the final manuscript and Colleen McKay for trekking around Tompkins Square Park and East 9th Street in the summer heat taking photographs of the neighborhood. There are really no words to express my gratitude to Margaret Randall, not only for her help with the manuscript and her Gabriela Mistral translation which begins the book, but most of all for her unwavering support and loving friendship through so many years. And, most especially, I would like to thank Bryce Milligan not only for believing in my work, but for all the endless hours and dedication he puts into Wings Press. A press I consider a great privilege to be represented by.

During my research, I came across the rather chilling fact that in the original version of "Snow White," the wicked queen was not Snow White's stepmother, she was her mother! It was evidently too controversial, so the Brothers Grimm changed it in their collection. Research on the Yiddish Theater is from Second Avenue Online, http://www.yap.cat.nyu.edu/ and research material and tours of original Lower East Side tenements is from the The Lower East Side Tenement Museum, 90 Orchard Street, New York City, 10002. http://www.tenement.org. The Chile chronology is from "The Guardian Unlimited/Special Reports" (link no longer available).

The phrases from "To Don Asterio Alarcón, Clocksmith of Valparaíso" are from Pablo Neruda, *Fully Empowered*, translated by Alastair Reid (The Noonday Press, a division of Farrar, Straus and Giroux: New York. 1975, pp. 63-65). The statue of the Monk Hoshi is the cover of *Parabola* (Summer 1981, Volume VI: No.3, "Mask and Metaphor: Role, Imagery, Disguise"). Catherine Riggs-Bergesen, who was the proprietor of the candle shop mentioned in "The Secret Heart of Clocks" is the author of *Candle Therapy* (Other Worldly Publishers: New York. 1993, 1999).

Some of these stories appeared previously in the magazines *Center* and *Local Knowledge*, and the chapbook *Casualties of War: New Poems & Prose* (Venom Press).

ABOUT THE CONTRIBUTORS
AND THE AUTHOR

Rona L. Holub is an historian, teacher, and the Director of the Women's History Graduate Program at Sarah Lawrence College. She specializes in women's history, urban/immigrant history, especially that of New York City. She earned her MA in Women's History from Sarah Lawrence College and her PhD in American History at Columbia University. She serves on the board of "All Out Arts: Fighting Prejudice Through the Arts" and is a licensed New York City Tour Guide.

Colleen McKay, a photographer and also a long time resident of the East Village, was the staff photographer for IKON magazine. Her photographs of Nicaragua, where she taught photo workshops in Bluefields in the '80s, were exhibited at the Henry Street Playhouse. Her photographs of writers, many used on their books covers, include Adrienne Rich, Audre Lorde, Hettie Jones, Blanche Weisen Cook, Gale Jackson, Josely Carvalho, and Kimiko Hahn.

Susan Sherman, a poet, playwright, essayist, editor and co-founder of IKON magazine, has been a resident of the Lower East Side/East Village, where she has been politically and artistically active, since 1961. In the Sixties she was poetry editor and a theater critic for the Village Voice and ran the open readings along with Allen Katzman and Carol Berge at the Metro Café. She traveled to Cuba in 1968 to attend the Cultural Congress of Havana and returned there for an extended stay a year later. She taught at the Free University of New York and the Alternate U., co-founded and edited IKON magazine and opened IKONbooks, a bookstore which served as a cultural and movement center.

In 1970 she was involved in the Fifth Street Women's Building squatter's action after which she became active in the feminist movement and the gay liberation movement. In 1971 she traveled to Chile while Allende was still in power, and in 1975 she taught at the feminist institute Sagaris. In 1984 she attended a conference on Central America in Nicaragua and revived IKON as a feminist magazine. After almost twenty years, she returned to Cuba in the Nineties as part of a feminist trip organized by Margaret Randall.

She has had twelve plays produced off-off-Broadway, has published seven collections of poetry and an adaptation of a Cuban play by Pepe Carril, *Shango de Ima* (Doubleday, 1971) which won eleven AUDELCO awards for a 1996 revival produced by the Nuyorican Poets Café. Her memoir *America's Child: A Woman's Journey through the Radical Sixties* (Curbstone: November 2007) has garnered critical acclaim from the *New York Times Book Review, Booklist, Publisher's Weekly* and *Lambda Book Review* and authors Grace Paley, Claribel Alegria and Chuck Wachtel. Her latest collection of poetry, *The Light that Puts an End to Dreams* (Wings Press, 2012), was a finalist for the Audre Lorde Poetry Award for Lesbian Poetry.

Her awards include a 1997 fellowship from the New York Foundation for the Arts for Creative Nonfiction Literature, a 1990 NYFA fellowship for Poetry, a Puffin Foundation Grant (1992), a Creative Artist's Public Service (CAPS) poetry grant (1966) and editors' awards from the Coordinating Council of Literary Magazines (CCLM) and the New York State Council on the Arts (NYSCA).

Among other periodicals and anthologies, her work has been published in *Changer L'Amérique: Anthologie de la Poésie Protestataire des USA (1980-1995), The Arc of Love, An Ear to the Ground, Poetry (Chicago), The American Poetry Review, The Nation, Conditions, A Gathering of the Tribes, El Corno Emplumado,* and *Heresies.*

She is currently working on a novel, *Deborah, My Song,* about three generations of women, and a new collection of poetry, *The Philosopher's Stone.* For more information about Susan Sherman, visit www.susansherman.com.

Colophon

This first edition of *Nirvana on Ninth Street*, by
Susan Sherman, has been printed on 55 pound
Edwards Brothers coated paper containing a
percentage of recycled fiber. Titles have been
set in Whiffy type, the text in Adobe Caslon
type. All Wings Press books are designed and
produced by Bryce Milligan.

On-line catalogue and ordering:
www.wingspress.com

Wings Press titles are distributed
to the trade by the
Independent Publishers Group
www.ipgbook.com
and in Europe by
www.gazellebookservices.co.uk

Also available as an ebook.